BUILDING *Trust*

ALSO BY KATIE O'CONNOR

<u>Contemporary Romance Series</u>

Heart's Haven:

Running Home

Saving Grace

Building Trust

<u>Contemporary Romance Single Title</u>

To a Tea

Rekindled Fire

Hearts in the Spotlight

<u>Erotic Romance/Erotica</u>

Stand Alone Erotic Romances:

Tessa's Trio

The Gift

<u>Covet the Cowboy Erotic Romance Series</u>

Corralling the Cowboy (Book 1)

Cornering the Cowgirl (Book 2)

Building *Trust*

A Heart's Haven Story

Katie O'Connor

Snarky Heart Press

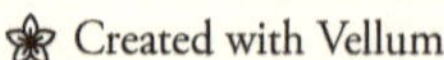 Created with Vellum

DEDICATION

*This one is for my agent, Dawn Dowdle.
Nobody has done more for my writing career than Dawn. Owner
of Blue Ridge Literary Agency, Dawn's gone the extra mile for me.
She's teaching me grammar and punctuation. She locates my plot
holes and helps me fill them. She negotiates and mediates on my
behalf. She works her tail off for me.
Dawn, thanks a million for everything you do for me and the other
authors you represent. We're blessed to have you guide us.*

CHAPTER 1

"Mommy, can Grampa come to daycare today?"

Lisa Brown looked up from tying her four-year-old daughter's sparkly pink runners and blinked until Amy's question registered.

"Why do you want Grampa at daycare?" A request to visit Amy's grandparents occurred almost daily, but for something so specific was uncommon. Unease rippled up Lisa's spine. This would be one of "those" conversations. She could almost feel it coming. Lord love a duck, she hated these no-win discussions. Times like this made her wish her husband, Davin, was still alive so she could pass the buck and make someone else solve the crisis.

"'Cause it's Father's Day soon, and everyone is bringing their dad to snack time today. And I don't have a daddy. Why don't I have a daddy?"

Good gravy. This morning, it was about having a daddy, and to think yesterday she'd been upset when Amy had rambled on about wanting a kitten they couldn't afford to feed. One thing about kids, they kept parents on their toes. Lisa sighed; so, this was why her friends sounded sarcastic when they joked on about the joys of motherhood. Mixed blessings.

"Oh, darling." Lisa knelt down and hugged Amy tightly. "You do have a daddy. He's just in heaven. I can come to snack today." Surely, her boss, Clint Dawson, would let her leave work for half an hour to visit the daycare. He wasn't a father, but he was one heck of an understanding man and often cut her way more slack than he probably should.

"You're not my daddy." Amy pushed out of Lisa's embrace and stomped her foot. "Why can't Grampa Brown or Grampa Dan come?"

"But Grampa wouldn't be your dad either. And they live a long way away." *God, grant me patience to deal with this.* Lisa resisted the urge to glance at her watch, knowing she was already late for work because she'd uncharacteristically slept in. She didn't need an argument right now; she needed to be out the door and on her way to the café.

"You're a girl, and it needs to be a boy. Some kids don't have dads, and they're bringing uncles." Tears brimmed in Amy's eyes, and her voice wobbled. Full-blown hysterics were seconds away. "I don't have an uncle or a dad. Why can't I have a dad? Other kids have a dad!"

Torn between frustration and anger, Lisa choked down the urge to throttle her daughter. And how had she missed the announcement of Father's Day snack? She should have prepared for this. God, why did Davin have to die when their only child was an infant? And why did kids unerringly find the worst possible moment to pitch a hissy fit? Life sucked sometimes. Being a widow was tough, but not usually unbearable. She searched frantically for a way out of this dilemma. Of course, the problem wouldn't exist if Davin were alive. What she needed here was a substitute, a pinch hitter.

"What if Mr. Clint came?"

"He's not my daddy." Amy sniffed and wiped a hand across her dripping nose smearing snot across her cheek. Her face brightened, and her frown morphed into a wobbly half-smile.

"No, he's not your daddy. But he is a boy." Lisa tried to grin. "He's my boss, and he was your daddy's friend. I'm sure he'd come because he loves you as much as I do." That much was true. Clint was Lisa's employer and one of her closest friends. He loved Amy like a daughter and was always ready to pitch in and lend a hand when Lisa needed him. He'd step up in a heartbeat.

"Let's call him." She pulled out her cell phone and dialed. Clint could usually be found in his office in the garage he owned, attached to the café where Lisa worked. The phone rang unanswered, so she tried the café.

"Hey, Clint," she said when he answered.

"Where are you? This place is a zoo. We've got a rig move stopped for a break. We're packed, and you're late. I called Bev in early. She'll be here in a half hour."

"I'm on my way, but I need a favor." She rushed on without letting him respond, saving time because they were moving an oil rig to a new location, and it involved dozens of trucks and even more rig workers. Heavy traffic like that meant the café would be swamped. "Amy needs a special man to come to daycare for the Father's Day snack later this afternoon. Do you think you could be there for her? We're kind of having a meltdown here." She hated the frantic pleading in her voice, but desperate times called for desperate measures.

"Tell her I'll be there and get your scrawny ass in here. We're swamped and I'm a shitty waitress." He sounded harried but not overly upset.

"Thanks so much. I'm on my way."

"Make it fast." The laughter in his voice was reassuring.

His patient, understanding and easy-going attitude made him a fabulous employer. She hung up and slid the phone into the pocket of her A-line denim skirt.

"Come on, Amy. Let's get you to daycare. Mr. Clint will be there for you today." Pulling a tissue from the box on the table, she wiped Amy's face.

"And next time, I'll have a real daddy?"

The hopeful look in those deep-brown eyes, so like Davin's, nearly broke Lisa's heart. "We'll see, baby girl. We'll see. But don't forget it takes a special man to be a daddy to a wonderful girl like you." She finished tying Amy's shoes and helped her slip into her jacket. "Grab your backpack. I'll drop you off at daycare, and Mr. Clint will come for snack."

CHAPTER 2

"Heya, boss." Lisa whirled into the café and snatched a black-and-red half-apron off the shelf behind the cash register. The restaurant was packed to the rafters, every table was filled, and almost all the chairs were full including the backups. The air was redolent with the mouth-watering aromas of bacon, sausages and coffee. Cups clattered on saucers, chatter and robust masculine laughter echoed through the room.

"You could have called earlier," Clint chided gently. He sidled past, coffeepot in hand. "Start taking orders. I've only got the three tables by the window done."

"I'm sorry about that. We were on the way out when all heck broke loose. I appreciate you stepping into Davin's shoes for the afternoon." She snatched up an order pad and headed onto the floor. She caught a glimpse of herself in the pie case mirror on the way past it. Her short, blonde hair stood out like crazy, her skirt was askew and her blouse half untucked. There wasn't a lick of makeup left on her face, except a smudge of mascara under one eye. She wiped it away with a napkin. Well, no time to worry about the rest of it now. She hurried to the first table to take their orders.

Two burly men sat across from each other, their impatience

showing. She flashed them her brightest smile of apology. "Sorry, guys. Family crisis with my daughter. What can I get you?"

They placed their orders; one man was pleasant, his partner, on the other hand, personified snippy and rude. She smiled broadly, despite their brusque attitude, thanked them for their patience and moved on to the next table. Behind her, she heard them grumbling.

"Service in here's slower than hell. She's got a job. What's her kid got to do with it? I just want my grub so we can get back on the road."

"Give her a break. Kids are a tough gig. Wait until your wife gives birth next month then you'll get it," the first guy said. "We aren't leaving until the rest of the crew is ready. So, suck it up. Drink your coffee. Enjoy the wait because we've got another ten hours to drive."

Forcing their conversation from her mind, she smiled brightly at the two men and the small girl sitting in the next booth. Thankfully, they already had coffee and chocolate milk.

"Hi. Sorry for the delay. Are you ready to order?"

"Daddy, I want pancakes," the little girl chirped.

"Pancakes it is. Sasha will have pancakes and bacon. I'll have the lumberjack special. Whole wheat toast, eggs over easy. Double bacon and no sausage, please. What'll you have, Cameron?"

Lisa turned toward the table's other occupant. Broad-shouldered, well-muscled and sinfully handsome, he took her breath away. His light brown hair needed a trim, and he had a five o'clock shadow, despite it being eight in the morning. His bright blue eyes sparkled at her. He winked broadly, and she shivered in delight. It had been a long time since anyone flirted with her. Haven just didn't have many eligible bachelors.

Abruptly, Cameron turned in his seat and glared at the grumbling occupants in the booth she'd just finished with. "Give the woman a break," he snapped. "She said she had a family problem. So, shut the hell up." They looked at him slack-jawed but didn't say anything.

He turned back and flashed Lisa another smile. "Sorry, Pixie-Sticks. I'll have the lumberjack special, too. Double sausage, double bacon, eggs scrambled, white toast and a side of fruit."

Struck momentarily brainless by his smile, Lisa stared at him dumbly. Gracious, he was hot, and he'd defended her. What a nice person.

"What? Er, pardon me?" she stammered and stared down at her notepad. God, those eyes were so sinful they made her melt.

Patiently, he repeated his order. "And a large glass of orange juice, please."

"Um. Sure thing. And thanks for sticking up for me," she whispered, so the men at the next table didn't hear. "I appreciate it."

"No worries, Pixie-Sticks. Nobody needs that crap."

She smiled gratefully at him. "I'll get this in right away."

She hurried from table to table taking orders and serving drinks. At some point, Bev, the second waitress, arrived and helped serve and run the cash register. They were rarely busy enough to need two, let alone three, waitstaff in addition to Clint pouring coffee and bussing dishes. A typical shift at the café included plenty of rest time between meals. Haven was a quiet town and her job easy, but today Lisa was grateful for the distraction from Amy's sudden interest in her father and especially from her own interest in the handsome man with those sinfully sexy blue eyes.

How chivalrous of him to defend her. A girl could get used to gallant kindness. She'd never seen him before. Wouldn't it be just her luck if he were simply passing through? The other man and the girl had been in a couple times, but she knew they weren't local. They were probably in Haven on vacation. In a town of a thousand people, give-or-take, you learned who the locals were pretty darn quickly.

Except for her boss, Clint, she hadn't had a man stick up for her since her husband died. Her time with Davin, God rest his soul, had been much too short. And while she was blessed to have such a lovely child, Davin's child, she missed having a man to stand by her side and to depend on. She shook her head to dispel the romantic vision. She was strong and independent and didn't need a man. She steadfastly ignored the part of her which still longed for a lifemate. And certainly, a blue-eyed, brown-haired rogue with a five o'clock shadow certainly wouldn't fit the bill. Even if she did want to kiss those luscious lips. Surprise at the thought had her stumbling across the floor. Was it lust?

No! Heck no! She was not lusting after some man she'd never even met. No way. No how. But those lips… She clamped down on the thought and pushed it out of her head.

Eventually, all the orders were delivered, and she had a moment to breathe. After a few sips of coffee, she was rejuvenated. Grabbing the pot, she worked her way through the restaurant, chatting with locals, smiling at strangers and making small talk with everyone. Mr. Five o'clock Shadow and his friend lingered over their breakfasts. She wandered Mr. Sexy's way to refill their cups.

"More orange juice?"

"No thanks, Pixie-Sticks." He winked broadly.

"Pixie-Sticks?" She gave him a puzzled look. What was with the weird name?

Nicknames were something you called a friend, not a stranger.

"You betcha." He winked again. "That spiky hair, those long, sexy legs, you remind me of a pixie."

"Cam, cut the s-e-x talk," his friend said, with a telling nod toward his daughter. "Little pitchers have big ears, and I'm not up to answering questions."

"Big ears?" the girl piped in. "I have small ears."

Cameron laughed. "She does pick up every little thing she hears, doesn't she?"

"Don't they all?" Lisa laughed. "My daughter never misses a trick."

"You have got a daughter?"

Lisa's gaze jerked back to Mr. Sexy Grin. What had the other guy called him? Oh ya, Cam. Cam sounded disappointed by her response.

"I do indeed. She's the love of my life. Even on days when she drives me to distraction."

"The love of your life? No man?" He glanced at her wedding rings with a raised eyebrow.

"Cam," the other man said pointedly.

"It's okay." Lisa smiled reassuringly. "I'm a widow."

"You know what they say about widows?" Cam waggled his eyebrows suggestively. His friend reached across the table and swatted him.

"No. What do they say?" Lisa planted her hands on her hips and glared. Jeepers, his crack was uncalled for. Who still believed that old stereotype anyway?

Cam coughed. "Um. Er. Nothing. They don't say anything." He looked down at his coffee cup, his face flushed. "I'm sorry."

She wanted to chide him for his rudeness. It was all she could do to keep a civil tongue in her head. Her job didn't pay much, and she needed every tip she could get to survive. "Can I get you anything else?" She ignored Cam and looked at his friend.

"Nothing, thanks. Just the bill, please. I'll take this jerk and get out of your hair."

She rummaged in her pocket then dropped their check on the table. "You can pay at the register. Thanks for coming in. Have a great day." Her voice was icy, but she didn't care. What kind of man categorized women by stereotype? And here, she'd thought he was cute. Pretty on the outside but ugly on the inside sprang to mind.

CHAPTER 3

"What the hell was that all about?"

Cam shrugged sheepishly at his best friend, Mark Sterling, as they left the café. They'd known each other for years. When they first met, their friend group had two Marks. Somehow, Mark Sterling had morphed into Sterling and years later, the nickname had stuck.

"She's hot. I thought she might be fun to date. But she's got a brat."

"A brat? Holy crap. You think Sasha's a brat?"

Embarrassment crept up his spine. "No. She's awesome. One of the best kids I've ever met. I love this little munchkin. She ranks right up there with my sister's kids." He ruffled Sasha's hair. Sterling had always had a knack for putting him on the spot with just a few words. If they weren't best friends, that ability would have driven him crazy. It was as if Sterling was Cam's conscience, his own personal Jiminy-freaking-Cricket.

"So why the widow bit? I'm a widower. Does that make me different?"

"I don't know. I was just…disappointed, I guess." Leave it to Sterling to make him feel like an ass. He already felt bad for being

11

rude. He still didn't know where the comment had come from. She'd caught his eyes the second she'd whirled into the café. The smile on her face had put the gleaming floors to shame. One look at her, and he was…disconcerted.

"Do you believe more women will date you if they think you're an ass?"

"Let it go, Sterl." Chagrin morphed into anger.

"If you liked her, you should've tried being nice to her, instead of implying she's a slut."

"She's not a slut. I didn't say that." He kicked at a small rock, sending it ricocheting across the parking lot.

"What the hell were you getting at? I mean, you're not one to be tied down, but you don't usually alienate women. Hell, ninety percent of your old flames are still your friends. The only one who isn't is Kim. But you come to town to visit us and act like a tool? What got into you?"

"I don't want to talk about Kim or dating." He dug out his keys, beeped his truck open then grabbed a folder from inside. "Here's the paperwork on the Harvest Heights development. Check it over and see how close I got. I think I'm getting a handle on writing up bids."

"I appreciate you bringing it from Calgary to Hicksville." Sterling laughed. "Haven is a micro-town, but the lake is great. Lots of parks and shallow water for Sasha. I'm staying here all summer, but I can't leave the office entirely. It means a lot that you're stepping in and filling my shoes while I'm gone."

"Daddy, the lady said there's a park out back. Can we go play there?"

Cameron and Sterling looked at each other and shrugged.

"Why not, Muffin?"

They locked their vehicles and wandered around to the back of the garage and café. There, nestled among a dozen urban camping spots, was a park. The sun-dappled area had swings, a climbing structure, a merry-go-round, two slides and a teeter-totter. Benches and tables sat sheltered in the shade of ancient pine trees close to the playground.

"You go play, and I'll check these papers. I'll come push you on the swings in a bit," Sterling said. They settled at a table, sitting side by side, so they could both watch Sterling's daughter. "Keep an eye on her while I look these over, will you?"

"You got it, boss."

"Partner. I'm not your boss. We're partners."

"I'm a silent partner. We both know my head for business sucks. I know which end of a hammer to hold, but my other skills are on life support." Cam was grateful Sterling had invited him to invest in Sterling Construction. He was great with his hands and good with supervising others, but he lacked a head for estimating jobs and dealing with unruly clients. Under Sterling's tutelage, he was learning, but he was content to be a silent partner.

The papers Sterling studied were Cam's fourth attempt at bidding a job alone and part of his learning curve. He was cautiously optimistic that he had done well. It had become their habit to have both of them prepare bids on the jobs Sterling Construction applied for. Sterling did the real bid, and Cam did a mock up then they compared them. Cam learned something new with every practice proposal. This time, he was sure he had it right. Maybe, Sterling would use Cameron's.

"This looks good." Sterling tapped the sheaf of papers. "But I'd make a couple minor changes. "See here? For the man hours, you've underestimated a bit. You're close, just a touch low." He went on to explain why he thought the number needed increasing. "You're short about five percent. Plus, I'd pad them a bit. Give us a bit of leeway in case of disaster…say an extra five percent. So, increase it by a total of ten percent. Then, I'd add a clause where we receive a bonus if we finish early."

"Isn't that grasping a bit? Being greedy?"

"It seems that way at first glance, but realistically, virtually no project is completed in the allotted time. Because they're in a hurry, it's in their best interest to agree to a bonus for early completion. It motivates us and benefits them in the end. They have the option of removing the clause if they don't like it."

"That makes sense."

"I also know this project has been put out to at least twenty-five companies for tender. We're unlikely to win the bid anyway. The early completion concept gives us a leg up over others. It's a good prospect, but we're not exactly hurting for work."

"I'll fix it up and email you a copy for final approval before I send it out." He kept his voice calm, but inside, he danced with excitement. Finally, after several tries, he'd completed a bid which met Sterling's tough requirements. Hot damn, it was good to measure up.

Silently, they watched Sasha play for a while. She was an adorable girl, tight blonde ringlets, sweet brown eyes and a ready smile. Cam loved his best friend's daughter. Watching her made him think of the waitress in the café. She had a child.

Was it a boy or a girl? He couldn't recall if she'd said either way. But damn, she was hot. Cute, perky, sexy. And that smile? Killer. If he had any intention of staying in town, he'd ask her out. He'd let her know the rules. A few dates, some fooling around and then he'd move on. But she had a kid. Women with kids didn't want flings. They wanted permanence, and he wasn't up for the commitment it entailed. He'd seen enough bad relationships to last a lifetime. He didn't need to get himself wrapped up in another one.

Nope, Pixie-Sticks would have to remain a fantasy, despite everyone knowing widows were hot and horny. A frown creased his brow. Why did it bother him to cast her in the role of horny widow? Did he feel bad because she'd complained? The idea of another man having her bugged him. Whatever it was, it left him feeling out of sorts.

Duty called, and he had to finish the paperwork and get that bid in on time. He said his goodbyes and headed for his truck. If he wasn't back to the city soon, he'd be late for his date tonight.

CHAPTER 4

"I can't believe you found your lost love only to find out he had a child with another woman. That has to suck." Lisa stared at her friend, Grace Winston. They'd been friends since Grace had moved to town a couple years ago. They shared every-thing. At least, Lisa shared everything. Grace didn't share her secrets. She didn't like to talk about her past much.

"Shh. Keep it down." They glanced around the nearly empty café. Nobody gave them more than a passing glance. "What the hell do I do?"

"Do you love him?" Lisa cut right to the chase.

"No. Maybe." Grace sighed and twisted her napkin between her fingers. "But he slept with her the night I left. It pisses me off."

"Come on, Grace. Stop with the melodramatics. You were friends back then. You weren't dating, and you had no claim on him. How can you judge him for what he did?" She sipped her coffee, tapped her fingers on the table and gave Grace a get-over-it look. Why was Grace getting so uptight about this? Time to break out the big guns.

"It's pretty simple, Grace. You either suck it up or end it right now."

"He slept with her." Grace dashed away her tears.

"And you didn't have a relationship with him back then." Lisa waved her hand dismissively. "You were friends."

"But I loved him."

"Oh my gosh. You've turned into a teenager. I've never seen you like this. You can't make a decision. You're weepy. You're jealous. Suck it up and admit you love him. Take it from someone who knows; you don't pass up love. It could disappear before you even know it."

Grace sighed moodily. "You make it sound so easy."

"Easy? Girl, love is never easy. It's painful, messy and it hurts. But it's worth every single second of pain and heartache. I still ache when I think of Davin. But he gave me Amy. His death sucked, but I've learned that everyone comes into our life for a purpose. Some good, some bad. You have to roll with the punches."

Why did Grace have such a block against love? Lord knew Lisa wanted nothing more than to find a good man to spend the rest of her life with. She ignored the mental image of Cam that jumped into her mind. She didn't want anything to do with a man with a huge ego. She just wanted someone warm, loving and dependable. Not some Lothario looking for a good time. She wanted what she'd had with Davin.

Yeah, having loved and lost sucked. Big time.

"But he—"

"Stop right there." Lisa held up a hand. "You ran away. You might have only been friends, but you dumped him. What was he supposed to do? Sit around and wait for you? Stop living?"

"Yes?" Grace blushed. "Okay, maybe not. But geez."

Lisa's laughter sparked an answering laugh in Grace.

"Okay, I get your point."

A shadow fell over the table, and someone stepped into Lisa's field of vision.

"Hey, Grace. How're things?" The man who'd defended her last month, stood there, looking all tall, dark-haired, and well-muscled.

Lisa recognized him immediately. Cameron. That whiskey voice, those eyes. Damn. Yeah, he'd stuck up for her…just before implying she was a slut.

"Hey, Cam. I'm good." Grace shifted over and patted the bench. "Sit. How's the guy who got hurt at the job?"

Cameron slid in beside Grace and wrapped her in a huge bear hug. "He's okay. He'll be on light duty. He can't run tools, but he can drive and run errands." He shrugged. "I say we let him go, but Sterl says otherwise."

"Just like that, you want to can someone?" Lisa huffed.

"Hi, Pixie-Sticks. How do you know Grace?" he queried Lisa.

"Pixie-Sticks?" Grace quirked one eyebrow then made introductions with a flourishing wave. "Lisa Brown, Cameron Zeus."

"Hi," Lisa responded coldly. She ignored Grace's questioning look.

"Hi, yourself." Cameron winked at Lisa then turned back to Grace. "What's up with Sterl? He left with you and came back all out of sorts. You're not messing with his head again, are you?" His words were teasing, but Lisa heard the unspoken warning behind them.

"We had a difference of opinion."

"He slept around on her," Lisa chimed in. "What kind of bastard does that?" She stuck up for her friend, despite not believing Sterling had actually wronged Grace. Friends stuck together, no matter what.

Cameron looked back and forth between them. "Ah. You did the math?"

"I did." Grace looked down and fiddled with her cup, and Lisa wished she was anywhere besides at this table. Grace was her friend. She wanted to stick up for her, to help her, but something about this man kept her quiet. It wasn't fear. It was more like…attraction. And a desperate desire to kiss him.

"Let me tell you this. You nearly killed him. I've never seen him so broken. He loved you like crazy, and you hurt him bad. He messed up and was just getting his shit back together when Marissa showed up. In the end, he did the right thing and kept their baby. Don't go all hoity-toity and rich-bitch on him now. He still loves you. He never stopped, though I don't know why. I would have…" He halted abruptly. "Never mind. My past has nothing to do with you guys. Just go easy on him. Okay?"

He rose from the booth, slid his hands into his jean pockets and stood there looking at them. "I missed you, Grace." He turned to Lisa. "Nice to see you again, Pixie-Sticks. See you around." He reached for her hand and kissed it lightly on the palm. "Later."

The soft touch of his lips sent a shiver up her arm and into her chest. Jeepers, how could such a casual touch wreak such havoc?

"What the hell?" Lisa stared after Cameron. He'd remembered her? They'd only interacted briefly that day at work, and he knew who she was? Wow. Maybe, she'd made an impression on him.

Grace laughed. "He's does love the ladies. He's an incorrigible, irrepressible flirt, but he's harmless."

"He's an ass," Lisa sputtered. An enticing, hot, sexy ass. Her eyes fixed on his muscular backside, clad in denim just tight enough to cling enticingly without being lewd or uncomfortable. She stared until he disappeared out the door. Reluctantly, she dragged her gaze back to her friend.

"Actually, he's one of the good guys."

"He kissed me, and he doesn't even know me." Bemusement filled her voice.

"He's a physical guy, always hugging someone. Where did you meet him?"

"At the café, I guess. He's vaguely familiar. I think." There was no way she'd admit she'd been fantasizing about him since she first met him. Who fantasized about a jerk like that? And she sure as heck wouldn't mention she couldn't read one of her treasured romance novels without seeing his face. And the dreams about his hands on her body? Nope. Not going to mention those, either.

They sipped their coffee without speaking for several minutes.

"So, whatcha gonna do?" Lisa pinned Grace with the question.

"I don't know. I'm stilled pissed off. But he did the right thing."

"And you didn't actually have a relationship." She waved her hand, stalling Grace's objection. "You were friends, not lovers, and he tried to find you." Lisa read Grace's reluctance to agree in her eyes.

"Everyone sticks up for him. His parents, his friends, my sisters. Doesn't anyone feel sorry for me?"

"Oh yeah, pity poor Grace. She's single, beautiful, runs a successful bookstore. She's got men tripping over their feet trying to date her. She's got such a tough life."

A bubble of laughter spilled out of Grace. "Okay, when you put it that way…"

"Let's not forget the man desperate to have you back in his life. How many guys would give someone they're dating access to their kid? I mean, if a guy was just using you, he'd keep you away from his daughter." It wasn't easy to date when you had a child to consider. Once upon a time, a casual fling might have been okay. Now, it was just out of the question. And in a small town like Haven, difficult became impossible.

"Dammit. My heart's on the line here. Stop being so logical."

"And leave you all wrapped up in misplaced emotion? Grace, you should be celebrating the fact that you've found each other and you have the chance to try again."

"I should?"

"You should!" Lisa laughed. "Starting over is a blessing. Embrace it with both hands. Grab onto him, hold on tight and don't let him get away." She reached out, grasped Grace's hands and squeezed them together. "He's gone out of his way to take a job here, near you. He's let you into Sasha's life. I've seen him around town, a lot. He seems like a wonderful guy. Don't let misplaced pride and hurt ruin something with the potential to be great for both of you. Let things take their course before you cut and run. Regrets can be brutal."

"That's what Nick said when I talked to him. He's my friend. I thought he might have some insight."

"You talked to Nick? How many people have you talked to about this?"

"Nick, Clint, you. And damned if you don't all agree."

"And you sit there doubting me?" Lisa waved her arm expansively and hid a grin at Grace's reluctant smile then picked up her coffee and swallowed the last few mouthfuls. Lord love a duck. People were stubborn. If she were prone to physical violence, she'd just smack Grace upside the head for being so blind to love.

Love wasn't easy. It was dirty, uncomfortable and messy. And heaven help her, she sure would like to get messy with Cameron. She choked on her coffee. Where had that thought come from?

"You okay?" Grace asked.

"Um." She coughed a couple times. "I'm good, but I better get back to work before Clint comes out and fires me."

"Yeah, 'cause Clint's going to fire his best waitress. Right."

They laughed together.

CHAPTER 5

isa raised her eyes to heaven and cast a silent prayer for patience. It was all she could do to keep a rein on her temper. Amy was back on the father issue. She hadn't let up for more than a few hours since the Father's Day event at her daycare. The argument was getting old. Fast.

"But I want a daddy. Why can't I have a daddy?" Nobody could whine like a four-year-old who'd decided they needed something. Lisa had known this day was coming, but heaven help her, she had hoped to delay it…for about twelve years.

"It doesn't work like that, Amy. You had a daddy. He's in heaven with the angels."

"Can he come back? I don't 'member him."

"Oh, sweetheart. God calls his most special people back to his side, and they go to heaven. We have to be happy God shared Daddy with us for a little while."

"Like Miss Emily makes us share toys at daycare?"

"Exactly. You are a very smart girl." She kissed Amy on the cheek and tucked her under the covers.

"When does it get to be my turn again?"

"Maybe, someday, you'll get a new daddy. But for now, we'll

just think about him in our hearts and be happy with what we have. And I am very happy to have you as a daughter. I love you to bits."

"I love you, Mommy."

Thankfully, Amy was drifting off. She was a bear to get into bed on a goodnight. But when she was overtired and needy, it was doubly difficult. Tonight seemed worse than usual.

"Goodnight, princess. I'll see you in the morning."

"Can we have pancakes?"

Lisa chuckled. What a kid. Always thinking of food. She pulled the quilt up tight against Amy's chin. "Yes, we can have pancakes." But Amy didn't hear the words, she was already fast asleep. Lisa crept out of the bedroom and eased the door shut. Time for a nice cup of tea and some quality alone time. Being a single mother wasn't an easy road to navigate, not even in a supportive town like Haven, making her relaxation even more precious.

Amy's sleepy request popped into Lisa's head as she steeped a pot of herbal tea. Pancakes. Kids and pancakes. Sasha had ordered them when Lisa had first seen Sterling, Sasha and Cameron in the café last month.

Cameron. She rolled his name around in her head. Cameron. Cam. Gracious, he was gorgeous. He'd been in the café again today. What was he doing back in town?

She mentally reran their second encounter. Working. He was working with Sterling, doing renovations on Nick's place. And he wanted to fire someone for getting hurt on the job. Was he serious? What kind of a jerk would fire someone for a mishap? Surely, he didn't mean it. It would suck if a glorious piece of manhood like him had a heart of stone.

Whoa. Wait. What was she doing thinking about his heart? She had no interest in his heart or any other part of him. She was a single mother, not a woman on the prowl. But man alive, it sure would be nice to cuddle up to those muscles of his or grab a piece of his very fine butt. Gracious, where were these lustful thoughts coming from? Thoughts like that would send her straight to hell. Clearly, she shouldn't have missed church last week.

She hadn't lusted for Davin like this. Life with Davin had been happy, serene and…comfortable. There had been no frantic heart pounding, no lascivious images haunting her dreams, interrupting her sleep. Life with her husband had been all she'd wanted and more. But now, she wondered if it hadn't been lacking something. Something she'd been unaware of.

She wasn't looking for lust. Was she? She carried her tea into the living room and settled down on the couch, legs tucked under her, a warm red, white and black crocheted afghan on her lap.

Would he stay in town long? It might be nice to see him again.

"Cameron. Cam," she whispered. It felt right. It felt strong and manly and perfect on her lips. And his lips… They looked firm and kissable.

"Stop it! Stop right now! You are not going there. Oh, good Lord, now I'm talking to myself."

Try as she might, Lisa couldn't banish the image of Cameron from her mind. Finally, she gave in and let her mind wander where it would.

In the morning, she woke with a kink in her neck from sleeping hunched over on the sofa. And to her dismay, Cameron was the first thing on her mind. This was not good.

CHAPTER 6

Lisa strapped on her running shoes and smiled at Grace.

"I appreciate you coming over to babysit. I've missed my run every day this week. I usually go after work, before I pick up Amy, but it's been insane between extra shifts and the rain. Have I mentioned how much I hate rain?"

Grace chuckled. "I love rain. Nobody has anything to do, so they bring their kids to the store. Rain is great for sales."

"I'm glad you're doing okay," Lisa agreed. "Last winter was tough on you."

"Yes, but I'm fine now. Go, run. Be free." She waved expansively toward the street. "Run yourself out. I've got no place to be until work tomorrow. In fact," she said grinning unrepentantly, "you should take some money and stop by Mulligans for a drink or grab a coffee someplace. Take your time; enjoy the evening."

"Nah, I'll just get a run in then come back. I've got my phone if Amy wakes up."

"Go. Shoo. Run like the wind. Be gone, woman. I've got this covered."

As she jogged away, she heard Grace call out, "And don't hurry back. You need a break."

Lisa slid her earbuds in and stepped up her pace. It took a few blocks for her to find her stride and run comfortably. She jogged through the center of town and down side streets until she hit the back road leading to the lake. She ran on the gravel shoulder, facing on-coming cars. It was a full mile before she achieved that mental place where breathing and stride meshed perfectly, and she felt like she could run forever.

Motion became automatic, and her body moved without conscious thought or effort, freeing her mind to wander. She did her best thinking when she ran. With her body on autopilot, her brain was free to run amok and find solutions to the problems that plagued her sub-conscious.

Today, it seemed everyone around her was in love, falling in love or getting married. She rejoiced for her friends, but in the dark moments which pestered her on occasion, she was jealous. Happily independent as a rule, she still yearned for a life-mate. A heart-stopping image of Cameron popped into her head, and she stumbled.

Four broken strides later, she regained her balance and plodded on, striving to find her equilibrium. She rounded a tree-lined corner, and in the distance, she saw another jogger. He ran with long, easy, ground-eating steps. Although vaguely familiar from the back, she couldn't identify him. Her competitive nature kicking in, she stretched her steps to close the gap in an effort to pass him.

Inch by inch, she drew closer. Seven hundred and fifty yards. Six hundred. Five hundred. The man paused to look over his shoulder before turning to run back toward town.

Recognition hit her like a rock. Cameron. It was as if her earlier thoughts had conjured him up. She jogged toward him, intending to continue past with only a nod. She was only twenty minutes into her workout and planned on doing a full hour. It had been entirely too long since she'd been out.

Cameron slowed his pace and flashed his sexy, rogue grin as she got close.

His lips moved, but she couldn't hear him over her music. She yanked out the earbuds and slowed to a stationary jog.

"Hi, Cameron."

"Lisa, I didn't realize you were a runner." He sounded impressed.

"On occasion," she replied, trying to calm her racing heart, but his proximity was playing havoc with her senses.

"Just on occasion?" he asked, his doubt clear. His eyes skimmed over her, leaving hot spots in their wake. "I would have guessed that you work out frequently."

"Thanks, I think. Running after Amy keeps me crazy busy, and I walk everywhere. I guess it pays off." She bit back a groan. This must be the most inept attempt at conversation she'd ever taken part in. He seemed to want to chat, and she just wanted to finish her workout. He was cute, but not for her.

"Well, gotta run," she joked and cast a tiny wave over her shoulder as she passed him.

She plodded on, her rhythm broken by the stop and her now persistent thoughts of Cameron. A motion beside her caught her unaware. Her heart exploded into action, and adrenaline spiked through her, leaving her fingers and toes tingling. The fight or flight response was instantaneous and involuntary.

As fast as the surge hit, she recognized Cam. He jogged beside her and winked when she glanced his way. She stumbled to a halt, planting her hands on her hips. A glare pinched her eyebrows together.

"Where are you going?" she demanded.

"Jogging with you?"

"Is that a question or an answer? You were headed the other way," she reminded him.

"It's a question and an answer, and yes, I was going the other way, but I've decided to tag along with you. The scenery is better this way."

His gaze caressed her legs, and he flicked her another smile.

"Why?"

"Somebody has to keep your beauty safe from the forest predators."

She rolled her eyes. "Seriously?" she asked, smirking despite herself.

"You're a mighty tasty-looking morsel. I wouldn't want to be responsible for a wild animal eating you up." His expression was somehow flirtatious, teasing and annoying, without making her uncomfortable.

"Do as you want. It's a free country." She struck out again, determined to ignore him. He followed beside her, silent for a few moments.

"So," he injected, "how long have you lived in Haven?"

"Four years, give or take."

"What brought you here?"

"I moved here with my husband. He worked at the garage before he passed away."

"I'm sorry you lost him."

She peeked over at him as they moved forward. "That might be the first nice thing you've said since we met."

"Really? I didn't think I was all bad. Well, except for the widow thing… Sorry. Sometimes, I speak without thinking. I meant no disrespect."

"What? The great Cameron Zeus made a mistake? Let the papers know," she teased.

"I guess I deserved that."

"Maybe."

"I'd like to buy you dinner," he suggested in an abrupt change of topic.

"What? Why?"

"Because I like you? Because you're cute? Because I'd like to get to know you?" He offered up a variety of suggestions.

"You're only in town temporarily," she hedged. "I don't see the point." Her breathing was getting heavy, and she realized she was pushing herself harder than she usually did on her runs. She wasn't trying to impress him, was she?

"True, but a man has to eat. You have to eat. Why eat alone when we can eat together?"

"I don't think so. I have a daughter I share meals with."

"Right, forgot about her for a second." They jogged on for a couple dozen paces. "Get a sitter. You must have one. You're out here without her." He looked triumphant and pleased with himself.

"True, but I think I'll still decline your generous offer."

Up ahead, she saw the sign for Radar Road, a side road to some local ranches which marked the three-mile point and her turn-around spot. She glanced around for oncoming vehicles then crossed the road to head back.

They moved together without speaking for close to two miles, Cameron matching his strides to hers. If she sped up, he did, too. When she slowed, he followed suit. As they passed the sign indicating Haven was a mile away, he spoke again.

"Okay, if dinner is out, how about I buy you a drink?"

"I'd still need a babysitter, so no thanks."

"You have a babysitter now. How about right now?"

"I'm sweaty and gross, so no thanks."

"You're glowing and quite lovely, so please join me."

"Why do you do that?"

"Do what?"

"Turn my words around and flirt continually. I've seen you in the café. You flirt with everyone. Why?"

"I suppose I do," he replied after a moment of thought. "I think all women need someone to flirt with them. It doesn't have to go anywhere. It just has to make them feel good and let them know they're important."

"So, you're trying to boost my fragile ego?"

"Are you always this difficult? We've been butting heads since the minute we met."

"No, I'm not. But you make me feel…disconcerted." She felt a blush creeping up her neck and coloring her already heated face. "Good grief, why did I say that?"

"I don't mean to make you uncomfortable. And frankly, you throw me off my stride, too. I don't know why, and but it makes me want to see you."

They were only a couple blocks from the bed and breakfast she knew he was staying at, and somehow, knowing they'd separate in a minute left her wanting more.

"Okay," she said. "You know where I live?"

He nodded.

"I figured you would. Haven's pretty small. Give me half an hour to clean up. I'll share a drink with you on my porch after I send Grace home." She waggled her finger at him in warning. "And I'm telling her you're coming over…so no funny business."

"Hell no. No funny business. Grace'd kick my ass. See you in half an hour and thank you." His smile was a mile wide as he jogged up the walkway to his temporary home.

CHAPTER 7

Cameron showered in record time and hurried to Haven's tiny liquor store for a bottle of wine. Inside the shop, he ran into Clint, Lisa's boss. He recognized him from the café.

"Hi," Clint said, stopping in front of the wine display, alongside Cam.

"Hi, how's your evening going?" Cam responded, wondering where this conversation was going.

"You know, Harmony doesn't allow alcohol in the rooms of her bed and breakfast," Clint informed him.

"I wasn't taking it there," he explained even as he wondered why he bothered.

"It's against the law to drink in the park," Clint persisted.

"I'm not going to the park. I have a date. Not that it's any of your business." He kept his tone level and unthreatening. Sterling had warned him small-town people kept track of each other.

"Lisa?" Clint asked mildly.

"How the hell did you know that?" Cam stared at him.

"I saw you jogging together earlier." Clint grinned. His smile morphed into something more serious and somewhat threatening.

"You be careful with Lisa. She seems tough, but she's got the softest heart I've ever known."

"Duly noted. I have no intention of hurting her. We're just going to have a drink and talk."

Clint looked him up and down as if assessing his soul and his intentions. Finally, he nodded. "Haven takes care of its own," he said picking up a bottle of chardonnay and handing it to Cam. "Lisa likes this one." He pivoted on his heel and strode away.

"Thanks," Cam called after him. "What does she snack on?"

"Salt and vinegar chips and dill pickle dip."

"Together?" Cam asked in disbelief. "That's crazy."

"Together," Clint confirmed, turning around to grin. "I said she had a soft heart. I didn't say anything about the relative insanity of her snack food choices. The store at the garage is open until eleven."

Cam purchased the wine and snacks then headed to Lisa's small house. It was cute, even if it was miniscule. It had clean, neat lines without much adornment. It was a bungalow, and unless he missed his guess, it dated from the late sixties. Recent updates gave it a modern feel. He wondered if they'd bothered to update the insulation when doing the renos. He hoped so. It got cold up here in the mountains, and good insulation was a must.

The house was painted a brickish red with white trim and a wide porch, complete with bent-willow chairs and a small, glass-topped table. Lisa sat under the overhang to the right of the front door. He strode up the steps to join her.

"Hi, thank you for having me. I brought wine and snacks." He thrust the bags at her like an awkward teenager on his first date.

"Thank you. I'll just pop inside and open the wine." She rose elegantly to her feet.

"You move like a ballerina," he blurted.

She laughed. "Thank you. Nervous?"

He chuckled. "Strangely, yes."

"Relax. I won't bite you," she teased.

"Isn't that supposed to be my line?" The gentle joshing helped him relax.

"I'm sure it's probably supposed to be yours, but for tonight, I'm calling dibs on it." She set the snacks on the table then sashayed into the house with the wine, easing the screen door shut behind her.

His gaze adhered to her hips until she disappeared from view. She was slender and graceful, reinforcing his initial impression of a pixie. He wasn't usually one for fanciful notions, but she made him feel…poetic. Sure, he was gifted with flattery and making a woman feel good about herself, but with Lisa, it was different. It was somehow important.

When she returned to the porch, he was still staring at the door.

She set the wine and two glasses down on the table. "This is my favorite wine," she said with a smile. "Good choice."

"I ran into Clint. He told me what to buy." Good gravy, he was losing his mind. Usually, he'd take credit for the choice. So why wasn't he tonight?

"You told him you were coming here?"

"Actually, he told me. I was standing in front of the wine, and he struck up a conversation. When I said I had a date, he knew it was you. He saw us jogging together. He chose the wine and the snacks. What kind of crazy person eats salt and vinegar chips and dill pickle dip?"

She chuckled. "Me. I grabbed a chip at a high school party and stuck it in the dip…and *voila!* An obsession was born. It's even carried over to chicken wings. I love to mix the two flavors together and have them with a ranch dip. And wings and sweet potato fries? Heaven on a plate."

"Ever had carrot fries?" he asked as he poured the wine and took a seat opposite the one she'd chosen.

"Carrot fries? Never."

"My neighbor's grandmother used to make them. And she

dipped slices of yam into melted butter, broiled them and served them with a mayo dip. Some kids craved cookies. I loved those damned carrot and yam chips."

"Davin's mom used to make this crazy dessert, sex in a pan. Cream cheese, pudding, graham crackers… It was sinful and to die for."

"I can top that. Warm brownies with ice cream and Irish cream liqueur dribbled over it. It was the only good thing that came out of my one long-term relationship."

She reached out and touched his arm. Her hand felt like a soft hug against his tense forearm. "I'm sorry she hurt you." Her compassion was unexpected but not surprising.

"Thank you, but I'm over her now." He cleared the lump lodged in his throat.

"I don't think you are over her, but for the sake of peace and since I hardly know you, I'm going to let it ride."

"Are you calling me a liar?" He bristled.

"No. Well, technically, I suppose I am, but that's not how I meant it. I meant I understand you went through a tough time and aren't ready to talk about her yet. I'm okay with that. It was a long time before I opened up about Davin and how much losing him hurt."

"Are you over him?" The softness and longing in Lisa's words made it obvious she wasn't over her husband.

"Yes and no." She laughed lightly.

He understood that her chuckle was directed at her ambivalence. "That clears it right up," he teased lightly. He sipped his wine. "This is good. I'm more a beer guy than a wine guy, but I don't mind this at all."

"Thanks, I like it. I much prefer wine to beer."

He watched her watching him and wondered what she was looking for. Finally, she spoke.

"I know we don't have a relationship, and it's early in our friendship to bring this up, but I'm going to anyway. I had a good marriage with Davin. I lost him too young, and I'll never get over that. I'll never stop loving him, which doesn't mean I'm not ready to move on and love again. The pain of loss, or in your case, betrayal, never goes away, but you learn to accept it, to live with it. There'll always be a hole where my husband was, but there's plenty of space for a new love." She scrunched up her eyebrows. "Does that make any sense?"

"It does, but it's too deep for a casual date." Part of him wondered if she was actually ready to move on, but there was no way on earth he'd pursue that line of questioning.

"And as for you," she said interrupting his thoughts. "You were hurt, and you probably have trust issues, explaining why you date a lot and treat it lightly. Me, I'm all about commitment and long term. I have to be. I have a daughter to look out for."

"You don't have any fun then?" He shifted in his seat and crossed his arms. Recognizing that his defensive pose could be mistaken for anger, he forced himself to relax.

"Don't be silly. I have a lot of fun. Laughing, joking and enjoying time with my friends are some of the best parts of my life, but dating is serious business. I can enjoy a date, not that Haven has many eligible bachelors, but… Never mind. It's too hard to explain." She picked up her glass and downed half of it in two swallows.

"A casual date is out unless I'm ready to commit to something long term?"

"A date is fine, but casual sex is out of the question. But yes, I'd prefer to date a man who wasn't afraid to consider a future together."

"What a pity. I don't do long term, and you don't do casual." He rose and stood before her. "Because you are beautiful, and intelligent and damned sexy." Leaning forward, he rested his hands on the arms of her chair and tilted until his lips were only inches from hers. "Goodnight, Lisa. Sleep well." He brushed a faint kiss across her lips, turned and strode down the sidewalk. He hopped into his truck without a backward glance.

Two blocks around the corner, he pulled up to the curb and killed the engine.

He flopped his head back, closed his eyes and willed his heart to slow down to a normal beat. What the hell? His heart pounded double-time, and he was as hard as a rock. He wanted nothing more than to turn around and join Lisa on the porch. He wanted, needed, to know everything about her, and for a brief moment, he'd forgotten all about his ex and the reasons he wouldn't consider commitment.

Lisa Brown was one of the kindest, gentlest women he'd ever met. She was spontaneous, funny and intelligent. In a nutshell, she was bad news, and he'd be well advised to keep away from her.

CHAPTER 8

*L*isa could hardly believe it was already the evening before Grace and Sterling's wedding. She smoothed her little black dress and knocked on the door of the doctor's house where the rehearsal dinner was being held. This would be the first time she'd been in Doc Hardy's home. She'd been in the offices out back more than once, but they had a separate entrance. She was curious to see what his home was like. Doc Hardy, she didn't even know his first name. Nobody used it. Everyone just called him Doc.

Tonight, she was nervous. Cameron would be here. Like her, he was part of Grace and Sterling's bridal party, but she wasn't looking forward to seeing him. Cameron hadn't been around much in recent months. Grace said he'd been closing down Sterling Construction's Calgary office. Sterling planned to base the company out of Haven once their city projects were completed.

When Cameron was here, he popped into the café, set her hormones on fire then disappeared again. It annoyed her that he had the power to churn up her emotions with nothing more than a few words and smoldering looks. No, she definitely wasn't looking forward to seeing him. A tiny part of her was tempted to skip the wedding altogether, but she'd never do that to Grace.

Tonight, Amy was at home with the babysitter. She'd wanted to be here, but it would be a long, late evening. Amy was having a sleepover with Sterling's daughter who was the flower girl. The sitter had strict instructions to get the two of them to bed early so there wouldn't be two overtired girls tomorrow.

Grace opened the door and yanked Lisa into her arms. "I'm so excited and nervous." She laughed. "What if Sterling changes his mind?" She twisted the edge of her sweater in her hands.

"Good grief." Lisa laughed. "After ten years of on-and-off relationships with him, you think he'll let you get away now? Not a chance. The man is smitten. He's head-over-heels in love with you."

For a moment, Lisa wished Cam was smitten with her. She liked him. A lot. But he had no desire to hang around Haven. And he sure as heck didn't want a long-term relationship. He'd made that clear on more than one occasion. Still, she'd never seen him on a date or heard of him dating anyone else. Of course, he spent a lot of time in the city.

She slammed the door on that convoluted thought path. She wouldn't let a man, any man, drive her crazy. She was content with her life, and when she was ready, the Lord would provide.

"I know, but our relationship has been so up and down..." Grace trailed off.

"Look deep inside. Look in your heart. Ignore that nagging voice in your head. Look deep, and you'll know he loves you. For now. For always. Sterling is totally gone gaga over you. This wedding is happening tomorrow, and the three of you will become a family. Forever."

Lisa didn't doubt their love. She saw it every time she looked at the three of them. Grace, Sterling and Sasha were a family and meant to be together. And while Sasha wasn't Grace's daughter, she sure looked like she was and Grace had taken her under her wing and into her heart. Yup, this was one family meant to be together.

She hugged Grace again. "Tomorrow will be the best day of your life. Stop worrying about it."

Grace laughed. "I can't help it."

"Is this a private hug, or can anyone get in on it?" Cam's voice startled them both.

"Cam. Come in." Grace stepped back, leaving room for him to enter the doctor's crowded foyer.

"Grace." He kissed her on the cheek.

He smiled warmly at Lisa and gave a flirtatious wink. "Lisa." He gave her an awkward peck on the cheek, making her blush.

MOLTEN HOT IMAGES of his nearly naked body gleaming with sweat assaulted her. They were followed quickly by lusty visions of his limbs entwined with hers, their lips locked together. *Oh glory. I have to stop thinking like this! And after one kiss? Crazy.*

"Come on, gals. Let's get this party started," Cam suggested and scooted past them into the house.

Laughing, they followed him into the dining room where the minister and the rest of the bridal party waited. Grace's twin sisters, Greta and Gabriella, looked lovely in elegant dresses. Sterling's friends, Nick, Cam and Clint looked fabulous in their casual button-down shirts and jeans. Wasn't it just like men to dress up just enough to get by while the women dressed to the nines? Sterling was handsome and charming in his suit as he scooped Grace into his arms and kissed her soundly.

"Stop fretting, Grace. I'm here. I'm not running, although I have thought about tying you down to make sure you don't make a great getaway again."

Everyone, including Grace, laughed.

"My running days are over. You're stuck with me now."

"Thank God."

"Amen," the minister chimed in. "Now, let's get this last run-through done so we can eat."

It took only ten minutes to have a dry run and to be sure everyone knew their roles for tomorrow's wedding. Doc disappeared into the kitchen and came back followed by the Ladies Auxiliary from the church who carried heaping bowls of food. The savory scents of basil, garlic, parmesan and meat sauce filled the over-crowded dining room. The spacious room was crowded with an extra table and enough chairs to fit the wedding party. Grace had debated having the dinner at Sid's but decided on something less formal and more intimate. The initial plan had been to have it at Sterling's, but Doc had offered his large home. Tonight was a gathering of friends to celebrate the upcoming wedding.

The ladies placed bowls of pasta and sauces on the table. There were several salads, fresh rolls and garlic bread. Desserts were heaped on the sideboard.

The minister gave a simple blessing to the meal, and they all dug in. In the shuffle to find seats, Cam had managed to seat himself between Lisa and Grace. His thigh burned hot against Lisa's, and she inched away. He shifted in his seat, bringing his leg back in contact with hers. She fumbled her fork, and it clattered loudly on her plate. In the din of the overfilled room, nobody noticed.

"Relax, Lisa. It's dinnertime, but I'm not going to eat you. Unless you want me to."

Snatching up her wine, she gulped down half a glass and shot him a glare. She didn't like where this was going. Was he really going to tease her and hope she fell into his trap? Well, two could play at that game.

She pressed her leg back against his, just slightly so he would think it was accidental. His answering smirk made her up her game. Her napkin fell to the floor, and she leaned down to pick it up, resting her right hand on his thigh and bending low, her head almost in his lap. His muscles shifted and tightened to hot iron under her hand.

Score one for the girls.

She stifled a laugh. Oh ya. She'd best him at his own game. Straightening in her chair, she smiled at him. "Sorry. Dropped my napkin."

"I'll bet you did." His eyes narrowed, and he searched her face as if looking for deception.

Well, he wouldn't find any telltale signs of a fib. She *had* dropped her napkin. She graced him with a quirky grin then turned her attention back to her dinner.

Everyone lingered over the scrumptious food, dessert and a few glasses of wine. Lisa and Cam played the game of besting each other's "accidental" touches, taking the teasing to new heights and greater daring. She rested her hand on his thigh, perilously close to his genitals. He sucked in a breath.

"Are you okay?" She gave him her best-concerned face and inched her hand higher.

"Fine." He choked out the word on a cough and swallowed hard.

"Oh good. I wouldn't want you to be uncomfortable." She traced the hard line of his thigh muscle with her fingertips.

He leaned in close, his breath tickling her ear. "You're playing a dangerous game, Pixie-Sticks. You'll regret teasing me." His tongue flicked out to catch the tip of her ear. "I'll get even, mark my words."

Her nipples pebbled at the touch and the threat.

"I see that," he whispered with a nod toward her chest. "You like it." He pushed back his chair and rose from the table.

"Are you finished?" a gray-haired serving lady asked him.

"I'm barely getting started." He chuckled. "But you can clear my plate. Thank you." She gave him a confused look and picked up his plate.

Following his lead, people began leaving the table to mingle in the living room.

Someone knocked on the door.

"Lisa, can you get the door?" the doctor called from the corner of the dining room. "I can't get out."

She nodded and went to the door. Opening it, she was surprised to see at least a dozen people on the front step.

"Um, hi," she greeted them. This was a private party, wasn't it?

"We're here to crash the party." Tamara, one of Grace's employees at the bookstore, laughed and pushed her way inside. The rest of the crew followed her. Lisa knew everyone, including the doctor's receptionist, Jessie.

"What's this?" Doc Hardy asked, pushing his way toward the door. "Tamara, Jessie, what are you doing here?"

"Crashing the party, boss," Jessie quipped and handed him a bottle of wine. Her red hair was artfully but messily piled atop her head, and she wore a pretty blue party dress.

He sighed heavily and winked at Lisa. "Haven. Nothing's a secret here. Why does every wedding turn into an over-the-top town event?" The question was rhetorical, and everyone knew it. Stepping to the left, he waved the party crashers inside.

More and more people arrived. Not once over the din of the party did Lisa hear anyone knocking. They just let themselves into the party. She was talking to Clint when his cell phone rang. He answered it, talked a minute then hung up.

"Can you tell Grace and Sterling I have to leave? Tow truck call. There's been an accident on Clive's Corner."

"Sure thing. Drive safe, boss."

He hustled out of the room.

It was a long while before he came back with a woman and her child. Jessie and Doc Hardy led them into the clinic in the back of the house after telling everyone the party was over. Gradually, the crowd thinned out until no one was left but Lisa and Cam, Grace and Sterling, and the Ladies Auxiliary who were busy cleaning up.

"Thank God, that's over." Sterling laughed. "Now, I can be alone with my bride."

"I'm not your bride yet." Grace teased, kissing him on

the cheek.

"Too bad, I'm taking you to my place for the night." He wrapped his arm around her waist. "Cam, take Lisa home." Scooping Grace into his arms, he carried her outside.

Cam took Lisa's hand and led her to his truck.

"You want me to ride in your work truck? In this dress?"

"That might be the sexiest dress I've ever seen." He flashed a come-hither grin. "Relax, Pixie-Sticks. Your dress is safe. I cleaned my truck today. Get in."

She checked out the interior warily. It was spotless, the dash shone and there was a clean quilt draped over the seat. She climbed into the cab and buckled up. He had her home in two minutes.

"I could have walked, you know."

"In those shoes?" He nodded at her spike-heeled sandals. "Those shoes are a man's wet dream. They're made for seduction, not walking."

She laughed. "Well, this is Haven. There aren't many places to wear shoes like this." She wiggled her feet. "When I get the chance, I wear them."

His answering smile was soft. He reached up and cupped the back of her neck in one hand. Leaning in, he whispered, "I'm going to kiss you goodnight."

His lips brushed against hers, as light as a breath.

"Goodnight, Lisa. Sweet dreams. Sleep well."

Hopping out of the truck, he jogged around to her side and opened the door. Although she didn't need it, she accepted his help out of the vehicle. Standing on the sidewalk, she looked up at him. Rising to her tiptoes, she pressed her lips against his.

"Goodnight, Cam. Thanks for the ride."

Before he could react, she turned and walked to her front door. She forced herself not to hurry, to keep her stride slow and seductive. She was torn between wanting to be in his arms and being safe, far away from him. Safety won over passion. Opening the door, she waved at him over her shoulder, without looking.

CHAPTER 9

The next afternoon, Cam hurried through the park, headed for the jumbo-sized, white tent housing Grace and the rest of her wedding party. He paused outside the pavilion to smooth his jacket and straighten his tie. The excited buzz of female voices filtered through the tent, too low to hear clearly. A carpeted runner led the way across the grass through rows of white chairs to where the minister and Sterling waited up front. Everything was bedecked in flowers with ribbons and bows. It was so girly and romantic he wanted to puke. Damn, weddings set him on edge. They reminded him of his broken engagement and Kim's betrayal. He just wanted this over and done with.

The music started, and Lisa stepped out of the tent. She smiled at him. He offered his arm. The sight of her took his breath away. She wore a knee-length dress that clung to her body in all the right places. It showed her tall, slender form to perfection. The damn dress should be illegal. Okay, maybe not, but nobody but him should see her in it.

The dress was some wild blue color. Sapphire, his mind told him. His sister had said the color wasn't blue; it was sapphire. Her crazy hair was spiked up, and she wore dangly silver earrings and a delicate silver necklace. She was the most kissable thing he'd ever seen.

"Come on, Cam," she whispered. "Grace is stressed enough without delaying this."

He shook his head as her words registered. He took her hand and tucked it in his elbow, holding it there with his. She was warm and soft and smelled like flowers. God, he wanted to bury his face in her neck and hair, suck up the delicious scent and memorize it. Forcing his mind to the job at hand, he led her up the aisle, knowing the rest of the wedding party followed.

He paused at the front while Lisa took her place then he moved to stand beside Sterling. He should have been watching everyone else, but Cam couldn't tear his gaze away from Lisa. What the hell was wrong with him? This wedding crap was turning his head to shit. Wedding ceremonies must have been invented by a woman determined to snag a man.

Weddings made women all goo-goo and turned a man's mind to things it shouldn't. Like love, permanence and commitment. A man just didn't need that kind of pressure. Dealing with women was enough on its own, without the romance.

The vows were interminable. Logically, he knew they'd lasted only minutes, but he just wanted to dance with Lisa, to hold her slender, delectable body against his. All he had to do now was survive the photographs and dinner. After that, at long last, there would be dancing. God, he needed a beer.

An hour and a half later, Cam stood behind the head table, wishing he'd planned this better. He had a vague idea where he wanted to go, what he wanted to say, but for some damn reason, the words vanished in a puff of flowery perfume when Lisa sat beside him.

Damn it all to hell and back.

He took a sip of his wine and cleared his throat. "Sterling, Grace, and all your friends... We came together today to witness a long overdue wedding."

Someone in the crowd shouted, "Hear Hear!" A good-natured chuckle echoed through the assembled guests.

"You were friends for years then, through a misunderstanding, lost each other. While that was tragic, it resulted in Sasha, and she is a gift. Fate brought Sterling to Haven where he found his long-lost love, Grace. The Lord saw fit to bring you back together. You're perfect alone, but together, you're more. All of us gathered here." He gestured around the park, "we're blessed to know you and be among your friends. You two have found something wonderful, something unique. You've found each other and became a family. May your life together be long, happy and filled with love." He raised his glass. "Tonight, I make a toast to Grace and Sterling, the most perfect couple I have ever known."

He touched glasses with the happy couple and turned to touch his glass to Lisa's. Her eyes glistened, and a lone tear slipped down her cheek.

Was she crying? What the hell? From his words? From something else?

Their glasses clinked together lightly, and they sipped, gazing into each other's eyes.

"Are you okay?" He kept his voice low. He didn't want to disturb anyone else.

"Yes. That was lovely. I didn't know you had it in you."

He felt his face flush, and he slid into his chair, momentarily breaking their gaze. "Yeah, me either." He chuckled.

"I thought you didn't believe in happily ever after."

"I didn't say that. I do believe in love. Just not for me." He picked up his fork and began eating. The creamy mashed potatoes could have been mud for all he noticed.

"You're wrong, you know." Her hand cupped his elbow. Her touch was soft and hot through his jacket. "There's love out there, for everyone. You just have to open your heart and mind to it."

~

LATE IN THE EVENING, Cameron stood on the edge of the sturdy wooden platform constructed for dancing and watched Lisa whirl around in Nick's arms. Jealousy swarmed through him. Nick had no right to hold her so close and have his lips so near her ear. He was probably inhaling her scent and thinking about kissing her.

"You should dance with her." He looked down at the old woman standing beside him. Gypsy Rose. She was a pip and a force to be reckoned with. She had her nose in everything that happened in Haven. She clutched a can of beer in one hand. No, wait, it was near-beer. He'd forgotten she couldn't see well enough to know the difference. Everyone in town was in on the doctor's plan to keep her away from alcohol since it interfered with her medications. Damn, for a visitor, he knew way too much about this town.

"You should cut in."

"Excuse me?" He glanced down at her. What was the old gal talking about?

"Dance with her. You know you want to. You can't stand to see her with another man. She's yours. You just won't admit it. You need to let go of past hurts and embrace the future. Get on with your life. She's not like your ex, you know."

"What the hell do you know about my ex?" He stared down at her.

"Just rumors. But I'm not called Gypsy for nothing. Whoever she was, she hurt you bad. But Lisa's not your ex. She's a good Christian woman with a big heart. She deserves to be loved. You either need to man up or walk away. Don't get her hopes up; don't break her heart." She shook her finger in his face.

"Mark my words, young man. You'll regret it if she gets away." With that bit of advice, she hobbled away, leaning heavily on her cane.

"She's right, you know." He looked to his left to find one of Grace's sisters standing there. He didn't know which one of the twins it was. He never could tell them apart.

"I'm Gabs," she said with a mock eye-roll, guessing his

dilemma. "Lisa's a doll, and for all your protestations, she's just what you need to get over Kim."

"Is there anyone on earth who doesn't know about Kim?" He glared around the dance floor.

"Besides Lisa? Probably not. You should tell her." She went up on her tiptoes and kissed his cheek then sashayed away. He watched her go. She was beautiful, intelligent and had a fabulous body, but she didn't move him in the least. She was like a sister to him. Lisa on the other hand…

Nick danced Lisa in Cam's direction. Stopping in front of Cameron, Nick released Lisa. "Cam, you better dance with her. My feet are killing me, and I need a beer."

Good grief. Was everyone hell-bent on hooking them up?

"It's okay. You don't have to dance with me." Lisa chuckled lightly.

"And let them nag even more. Fuck no."

"Language." She smiled, taking the edge off her admonishment.

"Come on, girl. Let's rock this joint." He grasped her hand and headed onto the floor. Without warning, the music turned to a slow, classic rock ballad. "Figures," he grumbled. There was no way he could win. The odds were stacked against him. Even the band had it in for him, so he took her in his arms and waltzed her onto the floor.

CHAPTER 10

*L*isa couldn't stop smiling as they danced away the rest of the evening. Slow songs, fast songs and everything in between. Cameron danced like a professional, with grace and rhythm to spare. He managed everything from casual dancing to polka to jitterbug, foxtrot and beyond. The man must have taken lessons at some point. Nobody was that gifted without putting some kind of effort into it. It was such a blessing that Grace had hired a couple teenage girls to watch over the children. Grace's stepdaughter, Sasha, Amy and a couple other youngsters were safely tucked away at a sleepover.

She was getting tired, and she'd had entirely too much wine. It was a blessing and a curse when the band started packing up their equipment. She wobbled her way to a chair and flopped gracelessly into it. She was perversely pleased when Cam followed her.

"My feet are killing me, but that was so much fun." She looked down at her feet. Her shoes were long since discarded. "Look." She lifted her leg and waggled her foot in his direction. "I've danced my nylons off."

Her dress slid up her thigh revealing the top of her stocking and the edge of her garter. She saw his gaze fasten on the little blue ribbon there, and heat blossomed through her. She should pull her dress down, but they were virtually alone, the revelers long gone except a few stragglers. Let him look. She watched him stare. In the dark of the late evening, she couldn't really see his eyes, but she felt his gaze burning against her leg. His Adam's apple bobbed as he swallowed hard. Longing darted through her.

"I need to find my shoes," she blurted and lurched to her feet.

"Where did you leave them? I'll get them."

"At the edge of the dance floor by the bandstand."

He jogged away and was back in seconds. She reached out to take her shoes from him.

"These are almost as hot as the ones you wore last night." He winked at her. "They give a man ideas. What is it with women and sexy shoes?"

"Give them back so I can go home, please."

"I have a better idea. Walk with me on the grass to the sidewalk. It'll be cool on your feet then I'll get my truck and drive you home."

"It's only a couple blocks." Good grief, she couldn't even protest convincingly. "I'll be fine."

"On sore feet? Besides, you've had too much wine to walk home alone." With her shoes in his left hand, he wrapped his right arm around her waist and led her toward the parking lot.

"This is Haven. There's nothing to worry about. I won't get lost, and nobody is around." She offered the weak protest, knowing he'd refuse her.

"A gentleman never lets a lady walk home unescorted."

"Ah, but we both know you're no gentleman."

His chuckle tickled down her spine. Hell's bells, she was drunker than she'd thought. Shit. Er, crap. Why did she discover curse words whenever she drank?

"Tonight, for you, I'm a gentleman. Wait here." He sprinted across the parking lot and returned with his truck. Opening her door, he lifted her inside and slid her onto the seat, placing her shoes at her feet.

He was warm and smelled heavenly. She wrapped her arms around his shoulders and pressed her face into the curve of his neck. So strong. So warm. So kissable.

"Whoa there, Pixie-Sticks. No kissing." He unwound her arms and closed the door.

"Don't you want to kiss me?" she purred when he climbed into the driver's seat.

"Don't go there." He kissed her nose and started the truck.

Her eyes drifted shut as she thought about the feel of his lips. The next thing she knew he was helping her out of the truck and up the front steps.

"Can you make it to bed alone?" He held out her shoes.

"Aren't you coming with me?" She clutched his arm.

"Not tonight. I don't sleep with women who've had too much." He walked her inside and down the hall.

She heard her shoes hit the floor beside the bed as he eased her down. He pulled a blanket up over her, whispered goodnight then disappeared.

Morning dawned way too bright and early. The sun streamed through Lisa's window, heating the room and warming her face. She'd forgotten to close the drapes last night.

"Oh God," she groaned. "What the heck was I thinking?" She rolled to a sitting position and climbed off the bed. She needed a shower something desperate. At least, she wasn't hung over. She'd been feeling good, but certainly not drunk. Just relaxed enough to ask for what she wanted.

And be denied.

Dang chivalrous man!

She didn't know if she should be pleased he'd walked away or annoyed. She stripped and slipped into the shower. She'd better get moving. She had to pick up Amy at the sitter's in an hour. As she soaped up, she said a silent thank you that Grace had been thoughtful enough to provide teenage babysitters for Sasha and Amy. At least, she hadn't had to deal with a rambunctious child this morning.

Stepping out of her shower, she heard the sound of someone in her kitchen. Who would be there this early? And how had they gotten in?

"When you're dressed, I brought coffee and bagels from Nick's Bakery." Cam's voice reverberated through her door.

Crap on toast.

She'd been hoping to avoid seeing him for a while. Days, maybe weeks, if she was really lucky. She hurried into some jeans and a T-shirt, towel-dried and fluffed her wet hair then headed for the kitchen. No sense delaying the inevitable.

"Hi. Gosh, that coffee smells good."

"I thought you might need a pick-me-up this morning." He smiled warmly at her. "How's your head?"

"Surprisingly good. I wasn't drunk, just tipsy." She hated the blush which rose in her cheeks. "And way too forward. I'm sorry for last night." She looked down into her coffee.

"No damage done."

"Thanks to you," she mumbled under her breath.

"I don't know what you think of me. I'm not in it for the long haul, but I don't take advantage either. I only play with women who want the same thing I do." His voice was curt and dismissive.

Shoot. She'd hurt his feelings. She gulped her coffee, scalding the roof of her mouth.

"Shit."

He gaped at her.

"Well, well, Polly Perfect cusses." His tone was sardonic, and when she looked at him, he had one eyebrow raised questioningly.

"Of course, I swear. And I drink too much on occasion. I never claimed to be perfect," she snapped.

"Isn't that just it? You never claimed to be perfect, but I'll be damned if you're not." He dropped his cup on the table. "Enjoy your coffee." He slid past her and out of the kitchen.

"Wait," she called after him. The front door shut quietly. "Damn."

Now, she'd pissed him off. And after such a lovely evening last night. Some days, it just didn't pay to get out of bed.

CHAPTER 11

$\mathcal{A}$ light knock sounded on Lisa's front door. She didn't bother to answer it. She knew who it was. The door opened and closed. Girls' night was about to begin!

"Hey, girl, we're here," Grace called out.

Lisa set an open bottle of white wine on the tray beside three glasses and a heaping bowl of salt and vinegar potato chips. She'd already taken the cheese, crackers, shrimp and dip into the living room. Picking up the tray, she joined her friends as they settled on the couch.

"Natalie, I'm glad you made it. I was worried you might bail." Natalie was new to town. She was shy and kept to herself a lot, but she was fast becoming a good friend to both Lisa and Grace.

Natalie laughed shyly. "I'll admit, I debated it. But Grace coerced Clint into babysitting." She blushed. "I feel bad leaving him with Mathew."

"Come on, don't be silly. Clint adores your boy. Just like he adores you," Grace teased.

"No! Don't say that. He can't like me. He's my friend. He's helping me out of a tight spot. That's all."

"Girl, you are so lying," Lisa teased. "He's hot and kind and generous. I'd take him for myself if he was at all my type and not my boss."

"Why isn't he your type?" Natalie sounded mystified.

"I don't know. He's got all the right qualifications, but he's just never interested me. Maybe it's because I knew him when I was married, and our friendship lasted. I mean, he's good-looking, but he just doesn't blow my skirt up. No zip; no tingles. Nothing special when he touches me. And he's never pushed for more than friendship, so I'm okay with that. He's all yours."

Grace spoke up. "I'm glad you came, Natalie. Lisa and I would have come over and dragged you out of the trailer if you didn't show up. I know you're hiding from something, but you're safe here in Haven. Plus, with us." Grace gestured to herself and Lisa, "you're among friends. And everyone needs to be with their friends."

"And you need time away from Mathew, and he needs time away from you. But next time, this is at your place so I can escape Amy. She's on the 'I need a pet' kick again. She thinks asking for a puppy instead of a kitten will make me cave. I swear that kid has pets on the brain."

"You should get her one," Grace suggested.

"I will when she's a bit older and less likely to hug it to death. But for now... Nope. Besides, I'm squirreling away every spare penny to get a car."

Natalie and Grace squealed with excitement.

"What are you going to get?" Grace asked.

"Something gently used that gets great gas mileage. Something I don't have to get a loan for. I can't afford payments and still save for Amy's college fund. I don't need a car often, but it feels too much like begging to have to borrow one on the rare occasion I need one."

"You know I don't mind lending you my car, and neither does Clint," Grace stated.

"I know that. But sometimes, I want to be independent and not have to borrow things. I'm making it on my own just fine, but…oh to heck with it. I can't explain it. Life's too complicated." She squished out a tiny laugh.

"Isn't it, though?" Natalie agreed. "Being independent is hard, but so worthwhile. At the same time, not having someone to rely on sucks."

Grace raised her glass. "On that note…a toast to being self-sufficient, independent and having a hot man to warm our beds and engage our hearts. Cheers."

Laughing, they clicked glasses together, and the conversation turned to things less serious. They talked about movies, books and play dates for a while.

"So, Lisa," Grace enquired, "when are you going on a date with Cam?"

"How about…the fifth of never?" Lisa wrinkled her nose. "He's not my type."

"Clint's not your type. Cam's not your type. Nick's not your type. Do you even have a type?" Natalie teased.

Lisa frowned and took a long swallow of her wine. Setting down the glass, she carefully stacked cheese and shrimp on a cracker and nibbled on it. When she looked up, her friends were motionless, studying her.

"What?"

"So, what's your type?" Grace asked.

"I don't know. Not a playboy, that's for sure."

"You do think Cam's hot then?"

Heat suffused Lisa's face. "I didn't say that."

Natalie crowed with laughter. "Look at her blush. She's totally into him."

"I am not." Her face got hotter. "I mean, he's cute. Okay, he's hot. But, I'm not into him. He's not the sticking around type. I've got a daughter, and I need someone I can depend on, not some horny Lothario."

"He is dependable," Grace said quietly. "But he was hurt in the past. Give him time to get over it."

"Well, if I'm single when he finally grows up, he can stop by. Until then, he can go play in someone else's sandbox."

Her friends gaped at her choice of words then all three women burst into laughter.

CHAPTER 12

The clatter of tools and whine of a power saw filled the air. The continual thunk-thunk of an air-nailer added to the din. It was as hot as sin, and thick, dark clouds filled the sky. They were in for a thunder boomer for sure and probably a downpour. They needed to get the plywood replaced on the roof before the rain hit. There wasn't any hope of getting shingles on, but plywood and tar paper would suffice for now.

Cam's attention should have been on the job, but for some reason, he couldn't get the image of Lisa out of his head. He should be working, not thinking about a little pixie of a woman with bright green eyes and pale pink lips that were always ready with a smile. Damn it all anyway. There was no way he'd get any work done while he was thinking about her.

Forcing his libido aside, he clambered up onto the roof, donned his fall protection and tied himself down. One more set of hands would get this place relatively waterproof until the storm arrived. Forty-five minutes later, the tar paper was firmly fastened down.

"Lunch time, boys." Cam slid down the ladder and brushed the sawdust off his pants.

Gradually, the din of the remodeling ceased.

"Early yet, isn't it?" Sterling's voice came from somewhere behind him.

"I'm starved," Cam defended as the rain started to fall. "Besides, we don't want to be up here in the rain. Too slippery. I'm headed to the café. Anyone coming?" Some of the guys carried bag lunches. Some went out to eat. It depended on the day.

"Thought we were headed to Mulligans?" Sterling stepped around the corner.

"Changed my mind." Cam shrugged in the direction of his business partner.

"I've got a craving for fish and chips." Sterling was referring to their alternate lunch destination, Mulligans' signature lunch special.

"And I've got a craving for the meatloaf special," Cam countered. "Go ahead. Eat fish." He shrugged as if it didn't make any difference to him where they ate. He ignored Sterling's knowing look.

"The café it is." Sterling's laughter grated on Cameron's nerves.

Ten minutes later, they stood inside the café door, watching the rain pour down and lightning flash. Thunder boomed off in the distance, coming closer with every rumble.

"What are you waiting for?" Sterling laughed. "To see which side Lisa's working?"

Cam glared at him. "I don't care who waits on me."

"Bullshit. You sit in her section every time we come here. Prove it and take a seat before you see her."

Irritation crawled up Cam's spine. Was it so unreasonable that he wanted to see Lisa? She was cute, friendly and as sexy as hell. He stomped across the café, pretending not to care where he sat or who their waitress was.

Motion caught Cam's eye. Lisa scurried from the kitchen, carefully balancing four plates. She walked to the far side of the room and set them on a table. Saved by the bell…er, waitress. Cam ignored Sterling, hurried to her section and slid into a booth.

"I knew it," Sterling teased. "You came here to see Lisa."

"I came here for the meatloaf special. They make damn good meatloaf here. She doesn't have anything to do with it." No way in hell would he admit he had the hots for Lisa.

"Yeah, that's why you waited until you saw her before you picked a seat. You've got it bad, buddy. Seriously bad. I've never seen you like this. Ask her out already."

"Ask who out?" Lisa strode up to the table.

"Nobody."

"You," Sterling replied at the same time.

"You're married to Grace." She pinned Sterling with a "naughty boy" look.

"I am. But this jerk," he said gesturing with his thumb, "has the hots for you but is too chicken to ask you out." He bobbed his head like a bird pecking the ground and made clucking noises.

She stammered a bit and dropped menus on the table. "What can I get you to drink?"

"Coffee, please."

"I'll have something tall and sweet like you, Pixie-Sticks." Cam winked.

Her brow furrowed, she glared at Cam.

"Iced tea, please." He flushed and looked down at the table. When he looked up, she was gone. Sterling chortled.

"You haven't figured it out yet, have you?"

"Figured what out?"

"Give me a freaking break. Lisa, you dipshit. You've got no idea that she's different. Your empty flattery won't get far with her. She's a single mother. She's probably not looking to date, and she sure won't be after a fling. You should back away."

Back away? The thought was like a two-by-four to the solar plexus. He rubbed his chest and gulped in a breath. What the hell? Walking away from a woman had never been an issue for him. So, why did the idea bother him? And what the hell would he do about it?

"Can we join you? This place is packed." Two of their employees stood alongside the table.

"Sure." Sterling slid over, and Cam followed suit.

When Lisa brought their drinks, it was all he could do to look at her and stammer out his order. She was messing with his head. Big time.

~

LISA RETURNED to the table to greet the two men joining Sterling and Cam. Now, Cam wasn't even talking to her? He was as crazy as a bed bug. She returned to the kitchen fuming. What the heck was wrong with him? She grabbed the additional drinks and returned to the table.

"Hi, I'm Steve." The bulky, dark-haired man smiled up at her, his blue eyes shining.

"Hi, Steve." She smiled back and set the drinks on the table. "I'm Lisa."

"Nice to meet you." He offered his hand.

His hand was rough and strong against her palm.

"Haven's quite the place." He winked. "It has an old-fashioned charm and the most beautiful waitresses."

She laughed lightly at his blatant flattery and ignored Cam's disgusted snort.

"I don't suppose you'd be interested in dinner tonight?" He sounded hopeful.

"Oh. My. I can't tonight. My daughter has ballet. Maybe, tomorrow?"

"Do your dating on your own damned time," Cam snapped.

Everyone turned to stare at him.

"This is my own time. I'm on my lunch break. Got a problem with that?" Steve stared at Cam, one eyebrow raised mockingly.

Lisa blanched. Oh no, this was bad. They weren't going to fight, were they? And why the heck did Cam care who Steve dated?

"Let me out," Cam snarled.

"As you wish, boss." Steve winked at Lisa and got up from the table, letting Cameron out of the small booth.

"What about your lunch?" Lisa watched him stomp away.

"I've lost my appetite," he snipped over his shoulder.

"Sorry." Steve slid back into the booth and graced Lisa with a heart-warming smile. "I didn't mean to step on his toes. Are you dating?"

"No!" she blurted and felt a blush crawl up her cheeks. "Um. That is… I'm not dating Cam. I would like to see you, though, if I can get a sitter." She scribbled her number on a scrap of paper from her pocket and handed it to him. "Call me."

When their orders came up, she delivered them with a smile. She placed a takeout box on the table. "Here's Cam's lunch. No sense in it going to waste."

"I'm not paying for it," the third man mumbled.

"You don't have to." She glared at him. "I've covered it."

"You don't have to do that," Sterling said. "I'll get it."

"It's not a problem. Just take it to him, please. I don't want him to go hungry on my account." She didn't want them to see her blush, so she dropped their bills on the table and hurried away.

Good gravy. Why were men so idiotically macho? That man would have let his friend go hungry because he was too cheap to pay for his meal. Sterling had offered to pay, and Steve hadn't said anything. But the other guy…gee whiz. Men could be ridiculously hard to understand. It must be too much testosterone or something.

By the time Lisa finished work, the weather had cleared, and she didn't need her umbrella for the walk to daycare to pick up Amy. Everything was soaked. Water dripped off eaves, and the light breeze carried droplets from the trees. The skies were clearing, and the sun was peeking through the remaining clouds. The air was heavy with the fresh scent of rain and wet grass. She ambled along, not in a real hurry. If she arrived too soon, she'd interrupt afternoon snack and Amy would be annoyed. No sense poking the bear. She dabbled in the puddles, unconcerned about the water on her sandals and naked feet.

Loud rumbling of an engine intruded on her thoughts, and a huge pickup truck with the Sterling Construction logo on the side roared up alongside her, splashing muddy water up her legs and all over the bottom of her broomstick skirt. She leapt back and glared at the truck. Before she could even think, Cam was out of the truck and beside her on the sidewalk.

"What the hell was that?" He shook his finger in her face.

"What was what?" She blinked stupidly at him.

"Why did you humiliate me by paying for my lunch?"

"Humiliate you? Are you insane? I did you a favor. You ordered it. Someone had to pay for it, and I did. I sent your lunch so you wouldn't go hungry after you stomped off in a hissy fit because Steve asked me out."

"I wasn't in a hissy fit." He towered over her, glaring.

Clearly, he was trying his best to intimidate her. Well, he had another think coming. She wasn't so easily cowed, and no man would make her feel bad for an act of kindness.

She jabbed him in the chest with one finger. "First, I did you a favor by paying for your meal. Second, I didn't want you to go hungry. Third, I can date whoever I want. Fourth, you have no right to try to run my life. And fifth, you splashed mud on my skirt." She punctuated each point with a sharp poke to his chest. "And sixth, screw you, asshole."

She swerved around him and resumed walking. She only traveled six steps when he grabbed her upper arm and spun her around.

"Don't walk away on me," he snapped.

She jerked her arm free and glared at him. "I'll do whatever I want. Back off, Cam. Leave me alone and stay out of my life." She pivoted on her heel and left. She heard him sputtering behind her, but he wasn't making any sense. His words were bit-off half-sentences at best. His inability to speak made her laugh.

It's a good thing she wasn't interested in him, because clearly, he was unhinged. Funny, he didn't scare her. He was just acting…weird.

Her thoughts flipped abruptly, and she thought longingly of her marriage. Gosh, she missed Davin and their easy camaraderie. But heaven help her, he'd never fascinated her or infuriated her like Cam. Now, that man had a way of getting under her skin and infiltrating her dreams. Those dreams had become entirely too steamy for her sanity. Sometimes, they were enough to make a good Christian girl blush. She wasn't a prude, but oh my… She fanned her face as she strode up the steps to the daycare.

Fifteen minutes later, when she returned to the street, Amy in hand, Cam still stood where she'd left him. She didn't want to encounter him again, but she needed to stop by the grocery store, and it was behind him. She sighed and kept walking.

They'd almost reached him when he spoke.

"I'm sorry."

She walked past him.

"Mommy, he said sorry. You're 'posed to forgive him."

She heard him chuckle. Why did kids pick the worst possible time to throw your words back in your face?

"It's not a true apology unless you know why you're apologizing," she reminded Amy, knowing he'd hear.

"I'm sorry I was rude in the café, and I'm sorry I manhandled you earlier."

She couldn't stop her hand from rubbing her arm where he'd grabbed her earlier.

"Jesus," he blurted. "Did I hurt you?"

"Don't swear," Amy and Lisa said in unison, turning back to glare at him.

He looked down at the ground and mumbled another apology. He looked up, his face flushed, his eyes apologetic. "I didn't mean to hurt you. I don't know what came over me. I've never manhandled a woman before. I'm sorry."

"I'm not hurt, just annoyed. You don't use force to get your way. Ever."

"That wasn't my intention. I am so sorry. I just wanted to talk to you. I panicked because you were walking away."

She heard the genuine regret in his voice, and she'd never seen him so aggressive or repentant. Perhaps, she'd overreacted a little.

"You're forgiven. This time. Please, don't ever touch me again."

As they walked away, she felt his eyes on her. Rounding the corner toward the grocery store, she risked a look back at him. His lifted one hand in what might be a wave or maybe a hopeless gesture. Dammit. Now, she felt bad for growling at him. The man had her all tangled up in knots. He might be cute—okay, he was as sexy as sin—but he wasn't dating material. He had fling written all over him. She had a child and a future to look out for. A fling just wasn't in the cards for her.

Now, Steve on the other hand… He'd been in the café several times, though he hadn't introduced himself until today. He was always polite and respectful. He was new to town, coming here to work for Sterling. She didn't know if the move was permanent, but he seemed like the kind of guy who'd stick around.

Too bad he wasn't sex on a stick like Cam.

 fter a few days' reprieve, the late summer rains were back. Lisa loved walking in the rain. If this wasn't a date, she would have left her umbrella home and wandered around, enjoying the cool, moist air. It wasn't raining hard. It was more a heavy mist, but she didn't want to show up for her date completely drenched. Rain would flatten her spiked hair and make her mascara run, and she'd arrive looking like a crazy raccoon. Good grief, just thinking about the image made her laugh. At Sid's Steakhouse, she collapsed her umbrella, flapping it a few times to shake off the excess water before she slipped through the door.

She loved the ambiance here. Thick, distorted glass windows in an ancient, wood building made it look like a relic from the outside. But inside, crisp, white-linen tablecloths covered the sturdy tables. The lighting was dim and romantic. And the food… Good lord, the food was amazing. Nothing short of five-star dining at Sid's. Sid took great pride in the quality of food and the excellent service her restaurant provided. Sid's Steakhouse would be a hot spot in the city. Here, in Haven, it was just Sid's and the best place to eat.

Steve stood in the foyer and smiled broadly at Lisa as she shed her coat. It had taken two weeks to find an evening convenient for both of them and for her babysitter.

She liked the way Steve's blue eyes sparkled when he smiled at her. It made her feel…important. Wanted. Broad-shouldered with dark hair, he was attractive and cuddly. He was strong and fit, too. Construction work made for a hard body. As a bonus, he'd always been polite in the café, and his workmates seemed to like him.

"Lisa, I'm glad you made it. I could have picked you up." He offered his hand.

She shook it, hoping for sparks. Nothing. It was like shaking hands with her brother…if she had a brother. Dang.

"Sorry I'm late. The babysitter was running behind. I appreciate the offer of a ride, but I prefer to walk."

"We could have walked together."

"I'll keep that in mind."

Steve laughed. "You do know this is Haven, population one thousand? It would only take me three minutes to find out where you live."

He had a point. "True enough," she replied. "But I'm old-fashioned. I grew up in the city, and first dates were always 'meet at a neutral place'. Old habits die hard, I guess."

"A beautiful woman can't be too careful, which is why I respected your request to meet here." He placed his hand on her back and led her to the hostess stand where a tall, reed-thin, redheaded woman stood. "My date's finally arrived. We're ready now."

"Hi, Lisa." Sid greeted her with a warm, welcoming smile.

"Sid. You've come down in the world." Lisa chuckled. "Hostess? You're slumming."

The restaurateur accepted the teasing with a grin. "A good boss can do all the jobs required of her staff. My hostess has the flu, so I'm doing double duty tonight. Let me show you to your table." In no time, they were settled in a cozy corner beside a large fireplace, menus and wine in hand.

"So, tell me a bit about Steve," Lisa asked as soon as Sid walked away. She grinned at his shocked expression.

"Um, there isn't much to tell," he stammered. "I wasn't expecting you to put me on the spot so quickly. Not much for small talk, are you?"

"Frankly, no. I'll go first, if it makes it easier for you. I'm Lisa Marie Brown. I'm twenty-four, and I have a pre-school aged daughter. I'm a widow. I used to live in the city, but I've come to love Haven. The sense of community and safety is wonderful." She shrugged. "Your turn."

"Lisa Marie, eh?"

"What can I say? Mom was a huge Presley fan, and Dad indulged her. Your turn."

"Steven Tyler Stallone."

"Aerosmith fans?" She laughed.

"Nope. Dad's name is Tyler. Mom's dad is Steven. I kind of wish they'd gone Tyler Steven, but too late now. Nobody teases this Stallone about his name anymore." He flexed his arms. "I'm much too tough for that."

"Anything you say, Rocky."

"Don't be dissing the name."

She snorted aloud at his mock threat. A sense of humor was good.

"Married?" she asked bluntly.

"Single. I've been single for two years. My ex-girlfriend left me for a lawyer. Claimed she was too good for a grunt laborer like me." He shrugged it off, but she saw the hurt in his eyes.

She reached out and patted his clenched hand. "No shame in good hard work. I spend my days as a waitress. It feeds Amy and me and keeps the bill collectors at bay. At night, I study."

"Study what?" He seemed genuinely interested.

"Animal behavior, right now. I'm taking an on-line correspondence course. I'd like to be a veterinarian's assistant someday. You know, when I grow up."

"You seem pretty grown up to me." He smiled enticingly.

"Are you hitting on me?" She frowned and fidgeted in her chair.

"Is that bad?" His smile drooped.

"Too fast. Way too fast. This is our first date."

"Sorry. I feel like I know you already. I've talked to you so many times at the café. It doesn't feel like a first date, but I'll nail down my enthusiasm."

"I'll accept your apology, despite the poor construction pun." She smiled softly. "I'm not used to dating. I've never really dated much."

"A pretty girl like you? I doubt it."

Heat rose in her cheeks. "I married my high school sweetie. He died a couple years ago. Haven isn't exactly a hotbed of eligible men looking to take on someone else's kid."

"Well, I'll count that as their loss and my gain." He raised his glass for a toast. "Here's to you and getting to know you better, without pushing my luck."

"I'll drink to that." They touched glasses, sharing a cautious smile.

"You'd better look at the menu before the server comes back for our order."

"Aren't you going to look?"

"Nope." She laughed lightly. "I'm having the New York steak with sweet potato fries and a garden salad."

"You didn't even look at the menu. I'm impressed."

"Don't be." She laughed. "I've been coming to Sid's forever. I pretty much know the menu by heart."

Lisa and Steve ordered the same meal, but while she ordered her steak medium rare, he ordered his blue rare. "You're an enigma," Steve said. "A lot of women don't eat steak."

"Okay, truth is, I don't eat much red meat. I'm partial to chicken and fish. But sometimes, I hear a steak calling my name." She cupped her ear with her hand. "Hear that? Yup, that's a steak begging me to eat it." She winked outrageously.

The steak was delicious; the sweet potato fries, crispy and steaming hot.

"Dinner was delicious. Thank you," she said as they finished their meal.

Steve smiled broadly at her words, clearly pleased she was happy. "Dessert?"

"Not for me but go ahead. I would like a cup of tea, though. I love a nice cup of Jasmine tea to finish off a meal."

"Shit. I mean, shoot," Steve exclaimed, looking toward the door.

"I don't need to have tea, if you need to go." His distress surprised her.

"It's not that. It's…"

"Lisa. Steve." Cam's voice was brusque and annoyed.

Lisa turned to look at him. "Cameron."

Tension radiated off him, from the rigid set of his shoulders to his hands fisted at his sides. Cam glared at Steve. "Fancy meeting you here."

"What business is it of yours where we go?" Lisa demanded.

"Did I say it was my business?" Cam snapped.

"You're acting like it's your business, when clearly, it isn't. Steve and I can go where we want and do whatever we feel like." She grasped Steve's hand from the table and held it between hers. Steve's gaze flicked nervously back and forth between her and Cam.

"Move along, Cameron." She flicked her fingers as if she were shooing away a fly. "What Steve and I do has nothing to do with you." She kissed Steve's knuckles.

He jerked his hand from hers and pushed his chair a few inches away from the table.

"Relax, Steve. We're not going to let this jerk ruin our lovely date."

"I think it's time to go," Steve blurted. "We're done eating anyway."

"But I wanted tea, and I thought you wanted dessert." He

wasn't going to let Cam push him around, was he? Didn't he have any guts at all? "Cam, move along. Go find a place to sit and leave us alone. And stop following me around."

"Following you around?" Cam snorted. "Like I give a shit where you go and who you do."

She felt everyone's eyes on them. Anger and embarrassment coursed through her. She jerked to her feet, her chair flying backward and tipping over behind her. She pivoted toward Cam and stabbed him in the chest with her finger. "Who I do? What the hell does that mean? Back off, jerk. Stay out of my life. And stay away from the café, too. You're no longer welcome there."

"You're banning me from the café? Are you insane? You can't do that." He grasped her finger and kept it from continuing to poke him. "I came in here for dinner, nothing more, nothing less. I don't give a shit what you do." He stormed off. "Don't be late for work tomorrow, Steve. Or you're canned."

She stomped up to Cam, grabbed his arm and jerked him around to face her. "What the hell is wrong with you? You're going to fire him for going on a date? You've got balls, I'll give you that. But you're an idiot. Leave him alone. Do you hear me?" She shook his arm. "Stop acting like a Neanderthal. Grow up and stop being an ass."

She glanced around the restaurant. Holy hockey stick! Everyone was staring at them, and Sid was bearing down on them, anger snapping in her eyes. Crap. What had she done? What had they done? They were causing a scene. She'd never caused a scene in her life. Dismay rocketed through her, and heat rose in her face. Good gravy.

"What the heck are you doing?" Sid growled. "Stop ruining my other patrons, evening. They came here for a nice, quiet dinner, not a floor show. Get out, and don't come back. Any of you." She waved toward the door. "Out. Now."

Steve fumbled for his wallet and dropped some bills on the table.

"Sorry." Lisa looked at Sid, hoping she would understand. "I'm sorry to cause a ruckus. It won't happen again."

"Goodnight, Lisa." Sid gestured toward the door again, hurrying them on their way.

Dismay washed over Lisa. She'd never made a public spectacle of herself before, nor had she been thrown out of a restaurant. She owed Sid an apology, a huge apology. She'd come back when it wasn't busy and beg for forgiveness.

CHAPTER 14

His dinner plans ruined, Cam followed the lovebirds into the parking lot. Thankfully, the earlier rain had stopped. At least, he didn't have to add a drenching to the insult of being thrown out of Sid's. Working in the misty rain all day had been bad enough. He was finally dry and wanted to stay that way.

"What the hell was that all about?" Lisa rounded on him and pinned him with a glare.

Her screeching set his nerves on edge. He was half-tempted to kiss her, just to shut her up, but one look at Steve's angry face squelched that thought. A fist fight over a woman who wasn't his was out of the question. Hell, a fist fight over any woman was out of the question.

"What was what about?" He played dumb.

"What the hell are you doing here, and why are you interrupting our date?" She crossed her arms over her chest, drawing his attention to her cleavage. She puffed out an annoyed breath, and her breasts heaved deliciously.

Oh yeah, she was pissed. Madder than a wet hen and just about the sexiest thing he'd ever seen. He was torn between calming her down and needling her further, just to watch her anger spike.

Something told him not to poke the bear; he might just get his head ripped off. Still, the temptation was there.

"I didn't come to interrupt your date. I had a hell of a day at work and came for a late dinner. Not that it's any of your business. I can't help it if you were busy making sickening goo-goo eyes at each other."

"Goo-goo eyes?" she barked.

"Walk away, Cam," Steve warned. "Before I do something I'll regret."

"Steve, don't even think of telling me what to do. And stay away from Lisa." The words were out before Cam knew what he was saying. His mouth snapped shut. Shit. Why did he say that?

"Stay away from Lisa?" Lisa echoed. "Who the heck are you to tell anyone to stay away from me? Back off, jerk-weed. Come on, Steve. Walk me home and keep me safe from this deranged idiot." She caught Steve's arm and turned her back on Cam. "And don't follow us, or I'll call the police."

Speechless, he watched them walk away. What was it about her that messed him up so badly? Why did he want her? He'd never felt this way before. Women were for fun and good times. Not once had he ever been possessive over a woman. Well, except for Kim. But his failed relationship with Kim was years ago, and he wasn't going back to serious dating. Ever. Not after what she'd done to him.

He stared after them until they'd disappeared around the corner. Should he follow them? Apologize? He didn't want her thinking badly of him. Why did he even care? Steve could go pound sand, but Lisa's frown plagued him.

"Jesus, man. You don't even know her. Why do you give a shit what she thinks?" he mumbled under his breath as he headed for his truck. He stood there, staring at the place where they'd disappeared, his chest tight and his arms tense. He was losing control and didn't like it. He rarely got bent out of shape and certainly not over a woman. His rationality had flown out the window.

The other day he'd grabbed her. Now, he was telling her who to date. He'd lost his frigging mind. He needed to see a shrink. He was losing his shit over a woman he barely knew.

It was true. He didn't know her. Not well, anyway. But he'd never had bad feelings with a woman before. He ignored his ugly break-up with Kim and her betrayal. Lisa was nothing like Kim. She was kind, generous and brimming with happiness. Everyone seemed to like her. And dear God, she was cute and adorable. Like a pixie. It nearly gutted him to see her with Steve. He didn't want to share her.

Share her? Hell, he didn't even have her, and he felt possessive? He'd been known to date more than one woman at a time. And he'd dated women who were seeing other guys, too. It had never been an issue. So why was it now when he wasn't even dating Lisa?

He climbed into his truck. Hopefully, he'd find food at Mulligans. And maybe a beer or three to drown his sorrows and help him forget about Lisa. He knew where she lived. He'd seen her in the yard with her daughter. Her house was in direct line between him and Mulligans. Screw that. He didn't want to see her snuggled up to Steve. He headed in the other direction, taking the long way around, ignoring the temptation to hassle them.

Mulligans' parking lot was jam-packed, and he had to park on the next street. He'd planned for a table to himself where he could nurse his beer and drown his sorrows, but with a local band playing, half the town was in the pub, and there was no chance of being alone. He wandered through the crowd, looking for familiar faces. He saw a wave from the back of the pub and shouldered his way through the crowd to join Sterling and Grace.

"This place is insane." Cam slid into an empty chair at their table. "Mind if I join you?"

"Pull up a stump. I thought you were heading to Sid's for dinner. At least, that's what Sterling told me." Grace sipped her wine and waved the waitress over.

"I was, but I ran into Lisa and Steve. Kind of ruined the evening for me," he confessed.

"Why don't you just ask her out? It'd be much easier than pining away for her. Trust me. I know about pining." Sterling laughed. "I spent too much time putting myself down and not enough chasing my dreams." He smiled fondly at Grace.

"Oh, God. Not you, too." Cam scraped his hand over his eyes. "I was hoping to escape all the lovey-dovey, goo-goo eyes shit. Can't a man just have a drink and some supper in peace?"

The waitress sidled up to the table.

"I'll have a double scotch, a beer, a cheeseburger, fries and a pound of hot wings. Please. You guys want anything?"

After the waitress left, Sterling gave Cam a penetrating look. "What crawled up your ass? A double scotch? And a beer? You never hit the hard stuff."

"Don't be silly, Sterling." Grace laughed and patted Cam's hand. "He's in lust. Again. And he knows Lisa's not the fling type. She's white picket fences and happily ever after. Definitely not the type for Cam."

"You've got that right. I'm not in it for the long haul. I'm only in town for this job."

"Why do you do that?" Grace queried. "You've been a horn dog as long as I've known you, and you always sell yourself short and avoid anything that even hints at long-term. At least, you have since Kim. She was years ago. You guys had issues and split up and you started dating anything that moved. Things change; life goes on. Stop letting your ex define you. You know you're a great guy and deserve long-term happiness with a woman? Right?" Grace's smile failed to take the sting out of her words.

"Not going to talk about this or about Kim."

"So, she cheated on you then dumped you. But not all women are like that. Some of us are honest and faithful. You need to give Lisa a chance. There could be more to her than you think. There's more to *you* than you think."

God, the last thing he needed was a lecture. He just wanted food and a goodnight's sleep. Why did women always interfere with a man's plans?

"Rein her in, Sterl. Let me eat in peace, and I'll get the hell out of here." Couldn't she just shut up and mind her own business. Grace was a great gal, but he sure didn't need her meddling. And the last thing he wanted was her pointing out things he didn't need to hear.

Grace laughed at his comment. When she was cheerful like this, Grace reminded him of Lisa. Dammit, why wouldn't Lisa stay out of his head? He just wanted to do this job and get back to the city. He didn't need the complication of a relationship.

A relationship?

Jesus, he'd gone from craving a fling to thinking about a relationship in seconds. He was losing his mind. Complete and utter insanity had set in. The goons in white suits would be after him any minute.

The waitress dropped off his drinks, and he downed the scotch in three quick swallows. With luck the booze would take the edge off and set his thinking straight.

"Let's just drop the subject of Lisa and relationships. I'll eat my dinner and leave you guys alone." Thankfully, they let it go and turned their attention to the music, letting him relax a bit.

An hour later, he left the pub and headed back toward the bed and breakfast. The night had grown chilly, and dark clouds obscured the moon. It smelled like rain. The air was heavy with moisture and something acrid.

Was that smoke? A forest fire? The province had been inundated with out-of-control wildfires. They'd only listed the fire ban recently.

Sirens and flashing lights came up behind him, startling him. He pulled to the side and let the fire truck pass. Up the street, it turned in the general direction of Lisa's house.

Rational thought fled, and he pulled away from the curb to

follow them around the corner and down the street. They stopped at a house that was fully engulfed in flames. He slammed the truck into park and bolted toward it.

Half a block later, he realized it wasn't Lisa's house. Relief flooded through him. It was the house beside hers. He relaxed slightly but stood frozen on the spot. It was too close to Lisa's. Was she okay? Was her daughter okay?

A second truck arrived and began spraying down neighboring houses, including Lisa's. He searched the crowd; if they were hosing down her house, she must be outside. Two firefighters led Lisa and her daughter out of their house and across a couple yards.

Halfway down the block, Lisa stood with her daughter cuddled in her arms. They'd been dragged from their house in their night-clothes. Lisa was barefoot wearing only a long T-shirt. Her daughter was in tiny, lightweight summer pajamas. He could almost see them trembling from here, despite the blanket a fireman wrapped around their shoulders. Turning on his heel, Cam ran back to his truck and grabbed a ragged quilt from the back seat. He jogged to them and standing behind Lisa, draped the blanket over her shoulders and wrapped it tight around her.

Shivers racked her body, and she didn't seem to notice he was there. She whispered quiet, nonsensical words of comfort to her daughter. The soothing tone of her voice calmed the crazy pounding of his heart. He'd nearly come unglued when he'd seen the fire.

Thank God, they were safe.

The fire blazed higher and higher despite the water being poured on it. Scorching air ripped the breath from his body. Firemen scurried back and forth. More sirens filled the air, and an ambulance careened around the corner coming to an abrupt halt. It was followed by an RCMP cruiser, its sirens wailing.

Police officers and firemen cordoned off the area, pushing people back and setting up barriers and ropes to keep the crowd at bay. Over the next few minutes, the crowd grew. It swelled in unison with the rising flames until it felt as if the night was on fire, the entire town watching it burn.

Slowly, the flames ebbed until nothing remained but a glowing hole in the ground, the stench of melted plastic and the acrid smell of ash heavy in the air. As the heat from the fire waned, Lisa's shivers increased.

"Come on, honey. Let's get you into my truck. I'll crank up the heater and warm you up."

She glanced at him surprised, as if she hadn't even realized he was there.

CHAPTER 15

"Cam?"

When had he gotten here? She looked down to discover she was wrapped in a blue-and-yellow quilt. His arms were around her, holding the quilt tight around her and Amy. He'd said something. What was it?

"What?"

"Come on; let's get you guys into my truck. I'll warm it up. You need to get out of the cold." His arms left her waist to wrap around her shoulders, edging her forward.

She stumbled a bit. Her feet seemed frozen to the ground. Shock, she must be in shock. This was unbelievable.

"No. I can't. I have to stay here." Panic crashed over her. She had to be here. She had to make sure her home was safe. "My house…"

"Your house is okay. Wet but okay." His voice was calm and reasonable. "But you're freezing. We have to warm up your daughter before she catches a chill."

"But the police…"

"I'll tell them where I'm taking you. We won't go far. See that truck, down there. We'll just go to my truck and warm you up."

85

"No. I have to stay." Why was he trying to drag her away? Her house was in danger; she could lose everything. She needed to stay here.

"Lisa. Look at me." His voice was curt. She pivoted to look into his eyes. "It's okay. Your house is fine. But your daughter is freezing. She's wet from the overspray from the hoses. We have to warm her up before she catches a cold."

She looked down at Amy. She was shivering despite being wrapped in the quilt and Lisa's arms. Gracious, he was right. They had to get warm. Now.

"Oh, Amy. Are you okay?"

"Mommy, I'm scareded. I'm c-c-cold."

"Come on, Amy, Lisa. Let's go to my truck and warm up."

She wouldn't relinquish Amy, but Lisa let him guide them down the street, trying not to stumble. He'd stopped to talk to one of the police officers, their voices too low to hear. Now, he opened the truck and loaded them inside. Amy sat in the middle, and Lisa sat on the outside. He shucked his jacket and wrapped it around Lisa's shoulders before closing the door. The coat was blessedly warm, and beneath the stench of fire, she smelled Cameron. The scent of coffee, sawdust and expensive cologne wrapped her in its embrace. She snuggled Amy under the jacket with her, rearranging the quilt for maximum coverage and tucking them both in as Cam climbed in on the other side.

"Th-th-thanks." Her teeth chattered.

"Hang on, I'll get this old beast running, and we'll have heat in no time. What the hell happened?"

"I don't know. I got home, and everything was quiet." No way would she mention Steve or the fact she hadn't let him come in. "I tucked Amy in, got undressed and climbed into bed. The next thing I knew I heard sirens and somebody was banging on the door."

She couldn't take her eyes away from the smoldering wreckage of her neighbors' house. "They aren't even home. They're in Europe for a couple weeks." Panic raced through her like rats on a sinking ship. "Oh my God. I'm watching their house while they're away. Oh my God. Oh my God." Her voice rose with each repetition and her hands flailed frantically.

"It's not your fault, Lisa. Relax."

"But…but…"

"But…nothing." His hand grasped hers and held them still. "It's okay. We'll find out what happened after the fire team investigates. Then you can call them if you want to. But if they have a lot a vacation left, you might want to let them enjoy it."

"What?" She stared at him. How could she not tell them right away? Sure, it would ruin their vacation, but they'd want to know. She'd want to know.

"I'm just saying it'll be bad enough for them… Why ruin their vacation?"

"They have to know. I'd want to know. They'll be so mad at me. I was supposed to watch the house." She heard the panic in her voice but couldn't stop it.

Amy reached up and patted her cheek. "Don't worry, Mommy. Just tell the truth. Everything works out if you tell the truth. That's what you tells me."

She stared down at her daughter and laughed. "That is what I say, isn't it?" She smiled. "Perhaps, you're right." She snuggled them back under the blanket and jacket.

A fireman knocked on the truck window. Cam lowered it a few inches.

"Hey, folks. We're still investigating, but it looks like there might be a leak in the gas line. We've shut the gas down for the entire area." He leaned in to look at Lisa. "You live next door, right?"

"We do. Why?"

"No gas for heat. You'll need to find a place to stay for at least one night. Sorry, ma'am. We'll let you know when you can go in and get a few things. But I wouldn't recommend staying long.

We're clearing a three-block radius." He nodded and walked away.

"Where the hell am I supposed to go?"

"Don't swear, Mommy. It's bad."

"Sorry, baby girl. I'll do better. But Mommy is really upset right now. We have to find a place to stay."

"That shouldn't be a problem, should it?" Cam asked.

"Are you crazy? This is Haven. There's no hotel and only one tiny bed and breakfast. There won't be rooms."

"Can't you stay with friends?"

"Everyone will be taking someone else in. This is a disaster."

"Objectively speaking, it's a disaster for your neighbors who lost their house. For you, it's an inconvenience. But you must have been scared to death."

Her jaw clenched. The man had balls, saying it was inconvenient. She opened her mouth to correct him, but it dawned on her, he was right. She snapped her mouth closed. Was she that selfish? Rationality set in. No, she wasn't selfish, just panicked.

"I'll make this easy on you. Come stay with me at the B&B."

"Are you insane?" He was hitting on her now? In front of her child? He had his nerve.

"Seriously. I've got two double beds. Grab some stuff and stay with me. I promise to keep my hands to myself. Hell, I won't even get undressed. It'll free up a room for someone else, and you'll be warm and dry."

"I don't know. I don't really know you. I have Amy to think about, too."

"And you need to think about your friends and neighbors."

The man was frustratingly logical.

"Who would you call first?"

"Clint or Grace. Why?"

"Call them, and tell them what happened, if they don't know already. Let them know you have a place and that they can use their rooms for someone else. They're emptying a three-block radius.

How many houses, how many displaced families with children? I'm offering you a place, so bigger homes have room for families with more children."

"I guess it could work, but I'm not sure I want to stay with you." Conflicting thoughts rampaged through her head. What was it that worried her so much? While she barely knew him, he'd almost always treated her with respect. Except when he was interrupting her dates. She still didn't know why he'd done that. But Grace and Sterling knew and liked him, and she trusted their judgment. Was she worried he was interested in her? Or maybe, that she was interested in him but not in a fling? Was she worried about becoming close to him and getting to know him better? Or was she just being overcautious?

She gave a mental shrug. Staying with Cam was an option, and it would free up space for her neighbors. She'd put her faith in Sterling and Grace's opinion of him.

"Okay. I'll do it." His broad smile annoyed her. "If you promise to keep your hands to yourself."

He crossed his heart. "Scout's honor."

She raised one eyebrow and glared. "Somehow, I doubt you were ever a Boy Scout, but I'm going to take you at your word. Don't make me regret it."

"Actually, I was a Boy Scout, and I received almost every merit badge. And I promise not to hurt you or kiss you…unless you want me to."

"Don't make me regret my decision." She shook her finger at him.

"I love that." He laughed.

"Love what? I have no idea what you're talking about."

He waved at her hand. "I love when you go all stern and mom-like. It's adorable."

"She's a doorbell?" Amy piped up.

"Not a doorbell." He chucked Amy under the chin. "Adorable. It means, sweet and cute and loveable."

"You love my mom?" she asked, wide-eyed in surprise. "But I don't even know you."

He coughed.

Was he hiding shock or a laugh? For the life of her, Lisa couldn't tell. He looked as if he'd swallowed something rotten. She chuckled.

"Um. Er. I like your mom. She's special," he blurted. "She's my friend."

Amy patted his cheek. "It's good to have friends 'cause then you have someone to play with. Mommy, I'm sleepy." She leaned back against Lisa and snuggled in.

Lisa pulled her daughter closer and tucked her in tight. The truck was warming up, and they'd finally stopped shivering. "Cuddle in, Baby Girl. Have a nap. We'll go to bed in a while. After they let us back in the house to get a few things." She kissed Amy on the head. "Love you."

"Love you." She trailed off sleepily.

"She's adorable," Cam whispered. "Outspoken like her mother, too."

"She's my heart. She kept me going when Davin died." Her heart clutched. God, she missed him, especially at times like this when her stress levels skyrocketed. Life wasn't fair when it took away someone you loved. Still, she was blessed to have such a lovely child.

"Davin was your husband?"

"He was. We were childhood sweethearts. He died in a freak accident at the garage when Amy was an infant." She hated thinking about it, about the pain and the fear. She missed him so much.

"Wow. You must be a trooper. Not everyone can deal with loss like that and survive it. I think you're handling things well."

"I had to. I had a baby to take care of. Sometimes, you just keep going when life hands you a pail of crap. You've got no choice, and you do what you have to."

"Well, I admire your strength."

She heard the conviction in his voice. His praise bolstered her mood. She didn't like to talk about her loss, but it was nice that someone recognized what she'd gone through and admired her for it. It wasn't so bad now, but looking back, she wondered how she'd managed to get through it. It was funny how you found the strength to get through the most unbearable events.

She fell silent. He kept looking at her, but he never spoke. What was going on in his mind? When would she get back into her house? How in heaven would she tell Gloria and Pete about their house?

She was tired and twitchy. Too much had happened today. The fight between Cameron and Steve. The fire. Being temporarily homeless. A silent scream of frustration choked her, stealing her breath. She felt a tear slip down her cheek. Would this day never end?

CHAPTER 16

$\mathcal{L}$isa had such an expressive face, and all her emotions flitted across it. After knowing her for a few months, Cam could read her like a book. Joy, sadness, stress, it was all there if you looked closely enough. He wasn't used to seeing Lisa so stressed out. Usually, she was so easygoing and always had a ready smile. Well, except for when he was annoying her. He did love when she got her hackles up. But now? He just wanted to pull her into his arms and hug away the sadness and exhaustion marring her pretty face.

A knock sounded on the truck window, making him jump.

Shit.

He rolled down the window to speak to the officer standing there.

"Miss, I'll escort you inside now. You can get a few things. I'll take your name and number, and we'll call you when it's safe to go back inside. Fortunately, while it's cold, it isn't below freezing, so you don't have to worry about burst pipes while you're without heat."

He looked back and forth between Cam and Lisa then focused his stare on Cam.

"You're not from around here, are you?" The officer asked.

He offered his hand. "Cameron Zeus. I work for Sterling Construction."

"How do you know Lisa?" His question landed somewhere between professional and a personal warning.

"I met him at the café, Mac," Lisa piped in. "He's a friend of Grace Winston's, er, Grace Sterling's. I keep forgetting she changed her name when she married Mark Sterling."

"You going to take her to the B&B?" There was a warning, maybe even a veiled threat, in his voice.

"I am. She'll be in room seven."

"In your room?" He fixed Cam with a no-nonsense stare.

Cam nodded.

"You okay with this, Lisa? I've got a spare room at my apartment. You don't have to stay with a stranger."

Cam's fists clenched. He resented the implication that Lisa might not be safe with him and wanted nothing more than to punch Officer Mac in the face. He sucked in a calming breath and closed his eyes. No sense getting arrested for reacting to an unintentional slight.

"McKenzie Stewart, stop being an ass. I wouldn't be in his truck if I didn't trust him. Save your bed for someone else. Heaven knows, there'll be enough people out in the cold."

Cam almost laughed when she leaned across him to shake her mom finger at Mac.

"We'll be fine with him." She turned to Cam. "Can you watch Amy? She's out cold and won't wake up until morning. I'd prefer to leave her here with you rather than lugging her inside."

Wow. She trusted him with her kid? Unbelievable. Pride swelled in his chest.

"Sure. We'll be fine. If she wakes up, I'll bring her inside."

"She won't. But thanks." She grasped his arm and gave him a peck on the cheek.

Her lips were soft and warm, and his arm tingled where she

touched him. Heat flooded through him. Damn. Turned on by a kiss of gratitude? One touch of her lips and he was hardening up like a teenager on his first date. This wasn't good.

She snuggled Amy in with the quilt, and still wearing his jacket, she headed for the house. She was tall and slender and looked fragile and vulnerable in his oversized jacket. It hung so long he could barely see the bottom of the T-shirt she wore for pajamas. And those legs… Geez, they went all the way up, and then some. He could almost feel them wrapped around his waist. He stiffened even more inside his jeans. Oh man, this was bad. She'd never trust him if he walked around with a hard-on all night. He had to get his mind out of the gutter before she got back.

He carried Amy and a suitcase into the B&B. Lisa followed him with a rolling suitcase, a tote bag brimming with toys and her purse. He hadn't realized how much stuff one kid needed. He'd been disappointed, but not surprised when Lisa had returned to the truck fully clothed. He'd kind of hoped she'd stay in her pajamas. No such luck.

He'd phoned the owner of the bed and breakfast, Harmony Farnsworth, and warned her he was bringing a guest. She met them at the door. The lobby was a big, open room with a fireplace burning brightly along one wall. The heavy drapes were drawn, keeping the heat inside. Three large couches surrounded the room, and four cushiony chairs had been bunched together haphazardly.

"Moving furniture, Harmony?" Cam teased.

"You bet. Mac called and said there'll be a lot of folks needing a space to sleep. I'm making room for cots. You folks head upstairs. I'll bring up a pot of tea and snacks for you, Lisa. You must be exhausted after all you've been through. And you, Cam, how nice of you to offer your room to them. Where are you staying?"

"I'll be with them. In case, they need something."

She gave him a penetrating stare. It felt as if she were reading his mind, searching for his intentions. Guilt washed over him. He was just helping out a friend; he didn't have any ulterior motives. Did he?

"I've got two beds."

"Don't you think I don't know that, you young pup? This is my place. When you've got her settled, come back down and give me a hand. I'll need some cots brought up from the basement. I'd best get ready for my extra guests." She walked away without waiting for his agreement. She was a pip. She reminded him of his grandmother.

The bed and breakfast was a converted, turn-of-the-century house. Harmony had her own suite. There was a big kitchen, a community sitting room, laundry facilities and seven guest quarters. Cam had taken one of the last rooms. The rest were filled with guests and other employees of Sterling Construction. He gave thanks that his space was the biggest Harmony had, with two double beds and a decent bathroom. There would be room for the three of them without trouble. He led Lisa upstairs and unlocked his door.

"I've been sleeping in the bed by the window. You guys can take the other one. If you pull back the covers, I'll slip Amy right into bed." Once the covers were back, he unwrapped her from the quilt and eased her gently onto the bed.

Lisa settled her in with a ragged stuffed dog and a small blanket before pulling up the covers.

"Can we leave a light on for her? I'm worried she might be scared if she wakes up in the dark in a strange place, even if I'm beside her."

"Sure. Would the bathroom light do? It won't bother me at all." He flipped on the light. "Help yourself to anything you need. Shower or bath, if you want to. I'll get Harmony to bring you a key so you can come and go as you need."

"Thanks. I might take a shower while you're out. I'm wired up and tense. This has been one hell of a night."

His gaze followed her to the door when she shucked his jacket and hung it inside the closet. Her exhaustion showed in her slow, jerky movements. She'd lost her natural grace. Her walk reminded him of a clumsy toddler instead of her usual ballerina elegance. A soft knock sounded on the door. Lisa looked at him for permission then opened it.

Harmony stood in the hallway with a tray with a pot of tea and a plate of baked goods. "Here you go, sweetheart. Get some rest." She smiled warmly then nodded toward Cam. "You, come with me. We've got work to do."

He suppressed a laugh. She was so obvious in her attempts to protect Lisa from him. He walked passed Lisa who stood in the doorway and dropped a kiss on her forehead. "Get some rest. I'll be as quiet as I can when I come back in."

AFTER TWO HOURS of rearranging furniture in what Harmony referred to as the parlor, he was exhausted. He'd moved couches and tables, hauled six heavy cots he was certain were antiques from the basement and toted eight loads of towels and blankets from upstairs. It was a lot after a long day of construction work. He didn't mind. It was nice to help people. After the heavy lifting was finished, he'd made coffee and tea and served some of the people who'd been ousted by the gas shut-off. He'd even made sandwiches and snacks.

The cots were full, and people were sleeping on the couches and the floor. The place was a zoo of individuals trying to get settled and whispering. This wasn't a tragedy. It was just an inconvenience, but it must be a real pain in the ass for those displaced. It was a blessing that the gas mains had frequent shut-off locations and not too many more families had been evacuated.

Blessings. Having Lisa in his room was a blessing. He might get a chance to get to know her better, to learn more about her and figure out why he was so attracted to her. She wasn't his usual type, not that he had a physical type. He'd dated everything from skinny to curvy and with every conceivable hair color and some colors that were clearly not natural. For Cameron, attitude was critical. He didn't much care for the Negative Nellie or the Sour Sally.

He liked a positive woman only in it for the short haul. Generally, he went more for the flingers than the long-termers. Sure, Lisa was cute and had a great body, but her clear desire for permanence should be off-putting. He didn't understand why it wasn't.

Being in Haven was changing him. First, there was his weird attraction to Lisa. Now, he was pitching in to help a bunch of strangers. It wasn't that he didn't have compassion, but he'd never done anything like this before. It wasn't how he was raised. Help for others had always been cash donations to charities rather than something hands-on. His family didn't lack money, and they were always willing to help financially, but to get down and dirty? This was something new.

There was something nice, something heart-warming about helping hands-on. He'd be doing this again. He liked the emotional payout. But damn, he was exhausted. He didn't know how Harmony kept going. When she'd shooed him upstairs to bed, she'd said she was headed into the kitchen to make cinnamon buns for tomorrow's breakfast. The woman was a dynamo.

He slipped into the room soundlessly and grabbed the sweats he'd left on the dresser earlier. A quick tooth brushing and face wash and he was ready to fall into bed. Closing the bathroom door to reduce the light, he snuck between the beds and eased down onto the edge of his. He sat for a moment, looking at Lisa and Amy curled up like two spoons in a drawer.

They looked like angels lying there together. He couldn't look away.

Lisa's arm was folded under her, her head resting on her elbow.

Her short pixie hair was still damp from a shower and stuck up every which way. It looked like it had been through a windstorm. She had a soft frown on her face and looked drained.

He stifled the urge to kiss her frown away. What could he do to ease her distress? How could he help? He'd never felt this useless before. He should be doing something, but for the life of him, he didn't know what that should be. He sighed softly, and her eyes opened.

"Are you going to stare at me all night?" She smiled.

"Um. No. Just thinking you look tired." He glanced away. She laughed, and he looked back.

"Gee, thanks." She smirked.

"I didn't mean it like that. You've had a rough evening. I'm sorry."

"Sorry for what? You didn't cause the fire. Did you?" Her light, teasing tone made him chuckle.

"No. But I was an ass earlier, and I apologize. It's not my place to dictate who you see. I just couldn't help myself."

"Apology accepted. Now, go to sleep." She wiggled around on the bed. One slender arm popped out of the covers to smooth them and pull them higher.

"You're beautiful, you know?" The words shocked him as much as they seemed to shock her.

"Um. Thanks?"

Even in the dim light, he saw her face flush. God, he was so tired he had no filter. Words popped into his head and out his mouth before they even registered. He'd better get into bed before he said something crazy or did something stupid like crawl over there and kiss her goodnight.

"You're welcome. Goodnight, Lisa. Sleep well. Sweet dreams."

"Goodnight, Cam. And thanks for being my knight in shining armor and rescuing us."

"Goodnight, Princess." He snorted at the image of him being anyone's savior and settled himself in bed. With luck, he'd be able to sleep in his sweats. It didn't seem right to sleep in anything less and certainly not in his usual naked state. He lay there facing her and watched her until long after her breathing had slowed and she'd relaxed into sleep. What was it about her was so fascinating? Why couldn't he stop thinking about her?

~

SOFT WHISPERS WOKE HIM.

"Where are we, Mommy?"

"Shh. You'll wake Cam," Lisa whispered. "We need to let him sleep. He was up very late helping Miss Harmony get ready for more guests."

He cracked open one eye to see them sitting up in bed, heads tipped together. They looked adorable. He ignored the streak of possessiveness flashing through him. He was not going to go there.

"Do we get to have breakfast with Miss Harmony? She makes the bestest cinmum buns."

"Yes, we do. Now, let's get up really quietly and get dressed; we can sneak out without waking Cam."

"Too late." Cam sat up then laughed when his guests both squealed in surprise.

"Jeepers, you scared ten years off my life." Lisa clutched her chest.

"Sorry. Don't worry about me. I'm an early riser. Why don't we get ready and go down to breakfast together?"

"Do you mind if I grab a quick shower first?" Lisa tugged the blanket up over her chest.

"Not at all. What do you think, Munchkin? Should Mommy do something with her crazy hair?" He winked at them.

Amy laughed. "She looks like a poke-you-pine."

"Funny. Very funny. I don't look like a porcupine, and I'm going to get you for that." She leaned in and tickled Amy until her giggles turned to squeals. After a couple minutes of relentless, delighted torture, Lisa kissed her daughter on the tip of her nose. "Mommy's going to shower. Be good for Cam. I love you."

"I love you, too, Mommy." She turned immediately to Cam. "Can we watch cartoons?"

He glanced at Lisa. She nodded her assent.

"Sure thing, Munchkin. What do you want to watch?"

She named a show he'd never heard of, and he spent the next fifteen minutes listening to shrill voices spewing the most inane dialog he'd ever heard. Kids' shows sure had changed since his day. Or maybe, he had. It didn't matter because Amy was happy and squealed with delight as she watched.

The bathroom door opened, and he looked up as Lisa came out. She wore a mid-thigh-length denim skirt, a snug purple T-shirt and funky beaded sandals. Her hair was primped back into its usual sexy mess, and she looked infinitely kissable.

Wow.

She laughed.

"Did I say that out loud?" He fidgeted under the covers.

"You did. Now, get yourself cleaned up. I'm starving."

He bolted out of bed and grabbed some clothes from the dresser. No sense showering, today would be another messy day at work. He grabbed a quick shave, brushed his teeth and combed his hair. By the time he left the bathroom, Lisa had Amy dressed and ready to go. She'd tidied up the beds, and all their stuff was stacked neatly on the desk.

"You sure work fast. I hardly recognize this place."

"Thanks. It's one of my mom skills. I know Harmony's going to be swamped today. I thought cleaning up a bit might make her life easier."

He liked Lisa's consideration for others, especially since she'd been ousted from her home, but "Mom Skills"? Shit. For a moment, he'd managed to push that fact out of his mind. Why'd she have to go and remind him? He forced a smile past his disappointment before he spoke.

"It's a ton of extra work for Harmony. Sterling's crew rented all her suites, but they were single occupancy. They doubled up last night. The old gal had me cleaning rooms for new guests. Last night, she took in at least a dozen people above full capacity. She's very generous. I'm amazed at her planning skills and how much work she got done last night in such a short time."

Lisa nodded her agreement. "She's insanely organized. She told me she could function at full capacity for two weeks in an emergency. You should see her root cellar and pantries. I'd guess she's got two hundred pounds of flour down there. When I asked about it, she said she needed it for baking."

"Speaking of baking, she was making cinnamon buns last night. We'd better hurry if we want some." Cam nodded toward the door in a let's-move motion.

"Breakfast time, kiddo." She tousled Amy's hair as they left the room.

Following them into the hall, he grabbed the Do Not Disturb sign and hung it on the outside of the door. "There. That'll keep her out." He snickered. "Kind of feels bad to trick the old gal."

"Who are you calling old?"

"Shit." He turned to face Harmony. "I didn't see you there."

"Watch your language in my home, young man. And I do appreciate not having to clean your room. I planned to leave it until last, just in case I ran out of time today. Now, I'll skip it altogether. Not that it needs cleaning every day. You're pretty tidy for a bachelor."

"My mother always complained about having to clean up after my father and me. I didn't get it until I had to clean my apartment when a date was coming over. I learned pretty quickly cleaning sucked, and if you didn't clean, you never saw that date again. I've learned to like things neat and tidy."

"So, you don't like it messy?" Lisa winked flirtatiously at him.

"Don't get the wrong idea." He held up his hands in a stop

motion. "Some things are meant to get messy. The messier, the better."

They stood there staring at each other, gazes locked together for one long moment.

Holy hell. His mind stalled for a second. Was she thinking what he was thinking? She couldn't be. She didn't seem the type. Not at all. Sure, she was the hottest woman he'd ever met, but to imply she liked it messy… Holy hell. He'd like to get messy with her. Steamy, hot, sweaty…

"You mean like making mud pies. That's supposed to be messy. But Mommy says I can't do it in my church clothes," Amy piped up.

Lisa and Harmony laughed.

Cam's mouth dropped open, and he choked. Where the hell was his head? Lisa was a mother first and foremost. And a good one from what he could tell. He had no business fantasizing about her. But man, her hot body, the sexy come-hither smile. Still, what was he doing having smutty thoughts about a good churchgoing woman? He'd burn in hell for what he was thinking, for the images flashing through his head. Bringing her to his room was a bad idea. It was beyond bad. It was insane.

He'd watched her sleeping for entirely too long last night. First, he'd wanted to crawl in and make love to her, but then, his thoughts had morphed. He wanted to hold her close, hug her and protect her. Protect her daughter. He'd lost his freaking mind.

Someone tugged on his hand. He looked down.

"Don't you think so?" Amy gave him a puzzled look.

"I'm sorry, pumpkin. I didn't hear what you said. I was thinking."

"And I know what you were thinking about." Harmony shook her finger under his nose. "Not in my house and not with a child present. You get yourself under control, mister, or I'll kick you out on the street." She glared at him and marched away.

"I said. You need to get dirty to make mud pies." Amy tugged on his hand, regaining his attention.

He laughed. "Indeed, you do, princess. You can't make mud pies without getting messy. One day, you and I will have to do that."

"Yay!" She jumped up and down, squealing excitedly.

"You know you've committed yourself, don't you?" Lisa asked dryly. "You have to watch what you say around kids. They never let any promise, no matter how vague, go unfulfilled. There's no backing out of it now."

"I guess I'll have to follow through then." He grinned unrepentantly, even as he wondered why the idea of making mud pies with Amy didn't bother him. He looked forward to it.

"You, my friend, are insane." Her eyebrows pinched together.

"You know what? I think I might be losing my mind, and I don't actually care." He reached out and smoothed her brow with his thumb. "Now, let's eat before I head to work."

CHAPTER 17

Lisa and Amy stayed with Cam for almost a week. It took only two days for the gas to be restored, but the fire chief wanted to finish investigating before allowing the neighbors immediately adjacent to the fire to move back home.

Lisa stepped out of the shower and wrapped herself in a towel. Amy was asleep in their bed. She didn't know where Cam was. He'd mentioned he'd be gone for a couple hours, and really, it was none of her business. Toweling off her hair, she wondered why she hadn't moved herself and Amy to stay with friends. Grace had room above her bookstore, and Sterling had a house now. Even Clint had space. Amy was easygoing and wouldn't object to the move.

"So why are we still here?" she asked her reflection as she ran a comb through her hair. "What's keeping me here?" The comb clattered to the counter. "Oh dear God. It isn't because I'm attracted to Cam, is it? Oh no. Heck no. Hell no!" She whispered the swear word. "Stop thinking about it. Another couple days and we'll be home and far away from his cute face."

She hung up her towel, slipped into her pajamas and left the bathroom.

"Did I hear you curse?" His voice came from out of nowhere.

She squealed in surprise and jumped back. Cam laughed.

"What are you doing here?" He sat in his bed, propped up on pillows, a paperback novel in his hand. His delectable chest was bare and called out to her lips. Gracious, she'd like to get her hands on that chest.

"Lisa?" His voice jolted her back to reality.

"What?"

"You're staring. Hell, girl. You're practically drooling. What's up?"

Her mind immediately slid into the gutter. What's up? She sure wished it was him. She could use a good dose of…

"Lisa!"

Her gaze snapped to his. Heat rose in her face. Dear Lord, she wasn't staring at his… Was she? She covered her eyes with her hand and stumbled toward the bed without looking.

"What's wrong? I heard you cursing in the bathroom?"

Her hand dropped, and she jerked around to stare at him. "You were eavesdropping on me?"

"Well, not intentionally." He laughed and winked. "But I couldn't help but overhear. The door to the bathroom is paper thin. So, you're attracted to me?"

"No!" She hopped into bed and turned her back to him. "Not in the least."

"Liar. I heard you. You can't go back on it now."

He chuckled quietly. Damn, he had such a sexy rumble of a laugh.

She sat up and glared at him. "Just because I thought it, doesn't mean I'll act on it. I'm a single mother with a child to deal with. The last thing I need is some vain, arrogant, womanizing jerk to get in the way."

"Womanizing? You think I'm a womanizer?"

"Yes."

"How long have I been in town?"

"How should I know?" She ignored the knowing look he gave her.

"I think you do know. I saw you for the first time when I visited in June. But for the record, I've been living here since August. It's October now. That's two and a half months, closer to three."

"Is there a point you're trying to make?" The embarrassment of being overheard was making her angry.

"How many women have I dated since I've arrived?"

Jeepers, she hated his calm, matter-of-fact tone. She shrugged, refusing to verbalize the answer.

"How many?" he repeated.

"Ten?" she asked flippantly.

"None. I haven't dated one single woman in the last three months."

"You're dating married women? Oh my gosh. That's awful." She glared at him and tugged the covers up higher, hiding herself.

"I haven't dated *anyone* since I met you."

"Well, you've been up to your neck in Nick's renovations." She wasn't flattered by his statement. Okay, maybe she was, but she sure wouldn't let him know.

"I work daytime hours. I have my evenings free. I'm not dating anyone. You've ruined me for other women." He glanced down, not meeting her eyes. "I have time to date. I just haven't met anyone to distract me from you."

"I'm not available." Oh gosh, did she really sound that prim and stiff? "I mean…" She stuttered to a halt, unable to form a coherent thought. Did he like her that much?

"I know you aren't available. You're a single mother and not the type I go for. I like fast and fun and carefree. Someone who enjoys life. No commitments."

Anger ratcheted up her spine. "I'm not fun? I don't enjoy life? Are you serious? I'll have you know I love life. I live life to the fullest, and I have a great sense of humor. Oh, you are such a… such a…man." She flopped down and turned away again.

"That isn't what I meant." His voice was soft and almost pleading. She stiffened but didn't sit back up.

"What I meant was I like you. You're smart, articulate, fun. You're beautiful and generous. You're a good person. I like you. Probably too much. But I'd like to get to know you better." He fell silent.

She rolled over but still didn't sit up. "Why?"

"That's the crux of it. I don't know why. You're everything I want, but at the same time, you're everything I don't want."

"Gee, thanks." She couldn't block the sarcasm from her voice. "Let's just drop this and go to sleep."

"I don't think I can." He was quiet for several long moments then finally huffed out a sigh. "Frankly, you make me want things I can't have. Like a long-term relationship. But I know those never work out. They just slowly suck the life out of everyone involved."

She bolted upright. "That's the stupidest thing I've ever heard." Her voice rose with each word. Amy stirred in her sleep, and Lisa placed one hand on her back, calming her. She forced herself to speak quietly. "Long-term relationships are based on love and understanding. They're beautiful and what life is about."

"Not in my experience." He scowled.

"Then you're looking in all the wrong places. I don't know what your ex did to taint your perception of love, but they're wrong. You're wrong. So very wrong. My parents were—no, *are*—happy. They have a great marriage. I had a great marriage." Sadness washed over her. "Or I did until Davin died."

"I'm sorry you had to lose him."

"Thank you. I still love him. I'll never stop loving him. But that doesn't mean I can't love again or that I won't ever re-find the happiness of true love and a long-term relationship. Somewhere out there is a man who can love me. Forever." It was true. She knew it. She'd find love again. Not with Cameron. He was too fast and easy and short term. But with someone. Too bad it couldn't be him because he made her heart race and her blood sing. He was sexy and masculine and funny. He had a good work ethic and was kind. He was blind to the blessings of love.

"Open your eyes. Open your heart." She dropped her voice to a whisper. "Love is out there, and it's good. You deserve more than just one-night stands. You deserve forever. Goodnight, Cam. Sleep well."

She pulled the covers up over her shoulders. Wrapping her arms around Amy, she closed her eyes and prayed for sleep, but it was a long time coming. Too many conflicting thoughts raced through her mind.

"Goodnight, Lisa." He clicked off the light.

In the darkness, with only a sliver of light from the bathroom for illumination, she watched him settle in. He lay still for a moment then shifted and rolled onto his side. He fluffed his pillow and lay back with his hands tucked behind his head. After a moment, he repositioned again. He pulled the covers up then pushed them back down. He wasn't having any more luck than she was at falling asleep. Good. He was wrong about love and long-term relationships. Let him stew. Let him wonder what he was missing out on.

CHAPTER 18

It became a habit for Cam to show up at the café every day for lunch during the week. Lisa didn't know where he ate supper or where he ate on the weekends. She lied and told herself she didn't care. But she could count on him coming for lunch Monday through Friday. He also had an annoying tendency to appear when she was grocery shopping or at the park with Amy. Seeing him was a pleasure and a curse. She liked him, but she didn't want to start anything with him. Short term was not her thing, and she doubted he was in it for the long haul.

Saturday morning dawned with the fall weather cool and cloudy. But at least it wasn't raining again. This was the wettest fall she could remember. Haven had been beset by rain for six days straight, and it was only a matter of time before rain turned to snow. Blizzards weren't far away. Amy was going stir crazy from being trapped indoors, and she was driving Lisa nuts in the process.

"Okay, kiddo. Get your coat and boots on. We're going to the park."

Amy's squeal of delight was deafening.

"Don't forget your wind pants."

"Is it windy?"

"No, silly goose. It's wet and muddy. Wind pants will keep the mud off your jeans. Some people call them splash pants." She tickled her daughter until they were both giggling breathlessly on the floor. Still laughing, they got dressed for their outing.

Her breath caught in her throat at the sight of a Sterling Construction truck parked on the street in front of her house. Her neighbors and several workmen were gathered inside the fence surrounding the remains of the burnt down house next door. She'd been wondering who would rebuild it since there was no longer a home builder in Haven. Thankfully, the Restinols had insurance, and the fire had been ruled an accident. Reconstruction could begin. In fact, it looked like it might start today.

Gloria and Pete Restinol called out a greeting. Dragging Cameron along, they walked up to Amy and Lisa. Gloria and Pete were complete opposites. Gloria was a whopping five feet eleven and as thin as a rail. Pete was five eight and generously rounded. Pete's balding head was countered by his wife's Texas-country-singer big-hair. They were an amusing sight but two of the most generous people Lisa had ever known.

"Morning, Lisa, Amy. Have you met Cameron? He'll be foreman on our rebuild."

Stifling a sigh, Lisa greeted them. "Let me tell you again how sorry I am your house burned down on my watch." She was sorry, despite it not being her fault.

"We just count ourselves lucky no one was hurt. Our cat, Muffin, came home today, too. He managed to escape somehow. I never thought I would be grateful for his escape artist tendencies." Gloria hugged Lisa.

"Our daughter had all our photo albums. She's scanning them and giving us digital copies." Pete chuckled. "We're just getting into the digital age and had our new camera with us. So, there is no big loss."

"How can you say that?" Lisa's jaw dropped then she snapped it shut. "You lost everything!" How could they be so calm and rational when their entire lives had gone up in smoke?

"We're safe. You're safe. We have our cat back and all our photographs and videos. Our important papers are in a safety deposit box at the bank. Everything else is replaceable." Gloria smiled sadly. "The whole thing sucks, but on the bright side, I get a brand-new house, a new wardrobe and entirely new furniture."

"She's been nagging for a new couch for six months." Pete chuckled.

"I'm glad it's working out. Sort of…" Lisa smiled and looked down at Amy who was tugging her arm, urging her toward the park. "Two shakes, kiddo."

"What's the big rush, Amy?" Cameron asked, completely ignoring Lisa.

"We're going to the park. I'm gonna make mud pies." She hopped up and down excitedly. "You should come."

"Sorry, princess. I'm working." He ruffled her hair.

"But I have my wind pants on and everything. And your pants are already dirty." Her voice was heavy with exasperation.

"True enough." He turned to the Restinols. "Any problem if I take a few minutes to play? We could meet at the café later. I'll bring the updated drawings, and you can make any changes you want. I was thinking we could expand the master closet a bit."

"That's an excellent idea. You go, play with Amy," Gloria urged.

"Don't you be playing matchmaker," Pete warned his wife.

Lisa laughed. "Come on. There's no stopping her. It doesn't matter that I'm not interested. She'll poke her nose in anyway. It's part of her charm—that and the fact she isn't disappointed when her evil plans fail."

"Evil? Why I never!" Gloria sputtered on a laugh.

"You do and often," Pete corrected her. "Your matchmaking attempts are legendary in town. Catch you folks later." He steered his wife toward their SUV.

"Is she always like that?" Cam gave Lisa a quizzical look.

"Ever since I've known her. She's had us over for dinner dozens of times. Usually, there's an eligible bachelor for company. She's pretty much tried to hook me up with every guy in town. I thought she'd given up on me. Times change when there's fresh meat I guess. And it'll get worse since they just finished their third honeymoon."

"Why do people in love always want to ruin everyone else's life by hooking them up?" Cam's nose scrunched up, making Lisa laugh.

"Misery loves company?"

"Come on. Let's go to the park." Amy grasped their hands and tugged them forward.

"Hang on a minute. I need to get something from my truck." He sprinted away and rummaged in the cab of his truck. He jogged back, brandishing a bag from the dollar store.

"What's that?" Amy asked hopefully.

"Ah, you have to wait until we get to the park to find out. Run ahead but stay in sight. We'll follow you."

Amy glanced at Lisa for permission then took off at her nod of approval. She got as far as the corner before stopping. She danced impatiently, waiting for help to cross the street.

"I'm sorry," Cam said quietly.

"For what?"

"For telling her to go ahead without asking you first. My sister would have killed me for that. Sometimes, I forget I'm not the boss." He shrugged.

"You have a sister?" Somehow, she'd never thought of him in terms of family or where he'd come from. He was such an entity in himself. "I thought you'd just sprung from the earth fully formed." She chuckled at the idea. "I never considered you might have relatives."

"I do."

"Details?" Was he seriously going to drop a random fact and

not elaborate? He must be out of his mind. There was no way she'd let it slide.

"My mom and my sister and her family. She's got three kids."

"That's it? No names? Genders? Husband?" Talking to him about anything personal was like pulling teeth. Painful and frustrating as all get-out.

"My mom and my sister are female," he joked.

She flashed him a warning glare.

"Angela is three years older than me. She's married to a guy, Jefferson, who she met in university. They're both teachers. Their kids are Randy, who's seven and Travis, who's four. And my favorite is eighteen-month-old Moxie. They live in Calgary near my mom. I visit them as often as I can. Ang is a great cook. She makes a melt-in-your-mouth roast beef and Yorkshire pudding to die for."

"I'll bet it's not as good as mine," she taunted.

"Is that an invitation to dinner?"

Wow, she'd put her foot in it this time. How could she extract herself gracefully?

"Sure. Next weekend?" The words popped out unbidden. Merciful heaven! What had she done? She'd invited him to dinner? What was she thinking? Okay, scratch that. She wasn't thinking at all. Nothing like getting yourself in a tough spot then digging the hole deeper.

He stopped in his tracks to look at her.

"Are you sure?" He raised one eyebrow. "You surprised me. You tend to avoid me."

Her mind selected and discarded several responses quickly. Oh sure, *now* her head got in the game.

"I've mellowed a bit. You're not so bad. You did take us in after the fire. Come over Friday night. About six. Just don't get the wrong idea. Friends. Nothing more. This isn't a date." She crossed her arms over her chest for emphasis.

"I've got a date with Lisa," he caroled in a singsong voice.

"Get it through your thick head right now. This. Is. Not. A.

Date. Not now. Not ever." She grabbed his arm, holding him back when he tried to skip away. "Not so fast, hot shot." She glared at his unrepentant smile.

"I've got a—"

"Don't." She shook her finger under his nose.

"You look like a schoolmarm when you do that." Leaning in, he kissed her nose then immediately leaned back, hands in the air in a surrender gesture. "Sorry. Couldn't help myself." Whirling away, he shouted over his shoulder. "Race you to the park." He scooped up Amy and dashed away.

She laughed and hurried to catch up. Why couldn't she stay mad at him? Was it his zest for life? Or her daughter's adoration of him? He had a kind side. If only he wasn't so set on a fling rather than a serious relationship.

She caught up with them at the edge of the sandbox.

"This is gonna be great." Cam knelt beside a huge puddle in the middle of the sand. "Tons of water and sand to make mud pies. Or better yet, a sand castle."

"I don't know how to make a castle." There was a hint of petulance in Amy's voice.

"No problem. I'll show you. We find some sand that's not too wet and not too dry. Squeeze it like this." He made a fist around some sand and opened it to reveal a clump that held together. "If it sticks together, it's perfect."

Amy tried, and the watery sand dribbled between her fingers.

"Good try. Not quite so wet. Try over here where there's less water. It takes a couple tries to get it right. Okay, got it?"

"I did it." She held up a solid ball triumphantly.

"Now, we use our hands to build mountains and dishes to build walls by packing the sand." He demonstrated both techniques. "Come on, Mom. Join us. Don't be afraid to get those angelic hands dirty." He chuckled as he dumped shiny new sand toys and cups from the bag he'd grabbed. "I bought these the other day, just in case I needed them."

He'd bought toys, just in case? She hadn't expected that.

She dropped to her knees in the sand beside them. Digging her fingers in the sand, she scooped and piled.

He was good with Amy, patient and understanding. He explained and showed her how to do it. That was nice. Not everyone had the knack for dealing with kids.

"I'll make a big hill to set the castle on." Lisa patted and piled until they had a platform suitable for a large castle. "Okay, now start building."

Together, they showed Amy how to pack the cups of sand, so they held together when the cup was removed. They showed her how to stack the blocks to build walls. It wasn't the best castle ever made. It was crooked and crumbling in spots, but Amy enjoyed every minute of building it.

"That was fun." Lisa leaned back on her heels.

"It's falling down," Amy whispered.

"That's what makes it perfect. Have you ever seen a real castle?" Cam asked.

"No. 'Cept on TV."

"Some of them are very old. Lots of them are falling down. This one looks real because it's falling down, like the big ones made of stones." He whipped out his phone and showed her some castle pictures. "I'll take some pictures and send them to your mom." He snapped off a few pictures of them. "Here, Lisa. Take a couple of Amy and me with the castle."

She took a few then joined them, taking a selfie of them all squished together and crouched down to fit the castle in.

"If you give me your email, I can send them to you. But first…" He jumped up and frantically piled sand. With the cups and shovels, he quickly assembled a ramshackle castle. "Okay, watch this." He leapt in the air and came crashing down on his creation. Roaring and growling, he stomped it into rubble. "I'm a dinosaur. I rule the earth." He roared at the sky and stomped some more.

Amy burst into laughter and joined him. She helped stomp his castle and, with a delighted giggle, kicked hers into oblivion. "Come on, Mommy. Be a dinosaur."

Lisa rose. "I'm a cat. Meow." She stepped delicately across the sandbox toward the swings. "Meow."

Glancing over her shoulder, she saw them staring at her as if she were out of her mind.

"Dinosaurs eat cats," Cam roared and chased after her.

"Don't eat Mommy," Amy squealed with glee.

They chased Lisa around the playground. Eventually, Cam caught her and dragged her to the ground, carefully cushioning her fall. She landed on top of him.

Laughing breathlessly, she stared down at him. He had a five o'clock shadow. He must have skipped shaving this morning. His blue eyes sparkled, and his grin was cheeky and sexy. Darn it. Why did he have to be so hot and attractive? But worse, why did he have to be so good with Amy?

He lifted his head infinitesimally. He was going to kiss her.

No way. She wouldn't kiss him.

Her mouth lowered.

His breath was a hot feather against her lips. His eyes darkened, his pupils dilated. Their hearts pounded in unison. His lips brushed across hers, barely skimming them, the touch almost too light to feel. Her heart stuttered then slammed into double-time beating. She wanted, needed to taste him. She crushed her lips against his. There was coffee, mint and man. Dear God, he tasted like heaven. His hand cupped the back of her head, drawing her closer. Beneath her, she felt him squirm and harden. Pressing back, she tested his desire.

This was such a bad idea.

It was delicious. He was delicious.

Her eyes drifted shut as his tongue tangled with hers. Desire blazing through her, she deepened the kiss. She wanted this. No, she wanted him. She hadn't been this aroused from a kiss since—

No!

Davin had never moved her like this.

She jerked away and sprang to her feet. Backing away slowly, she tried to clear her head.

She'd been making out with him in front of her daughter. She was losing her mind.

What the hell? Oh geez, now he had her swearing in her head. Who was this man? He was temptation incarnate. She didn't want him!

Liar. You want him. Badly.

One kiss and she wanted him more than the man she'd loved and married. It didn't make sense.

"I'm sorry. Lisa, I'm so sorry."

"Don't." She made a stop motion with her hand. "This was a mistake. Forget it ever happened. It will never happen again." Please, let him think she didn't want this. Even as she cast the silent prayer, her mind called her a liar again. She *did* want him despite their differing views on relationships. She wanted him physically, emotionally and on some deeper level…permanently.

"This was not a mistake. We're adults, two consenting adults who want each other." He scrubbed a hand over his face. "God, I can't remember the last time I've wanted someone as badly as I want you. I don't get it. You've bewitched me."

"I didn't…"

He inched toward her. "Of course, you didn't. There's no such thing as bewitching. But damn—er darn—there's something about you…"

"Stop. Don't say another word. This…this…whatever it is…is over. Walk away, and don't come back." As an afterthought, she added, "Please."

"Lisa." He held up one hand then dropped it helplessly to his side.

"Stop."

"Mommy, why are you yelling at Mr. Cam?"

Startled, she pivoted to glance at Amy. Her daughter looked bewildered; her brows scrunched up in confusion.

"Sorry, Amy. I'm a bit upset."

"'Cause he kissed you?"

"That's right, Amy." Cam shrugged. "I was wrong to kiss your mommy without asking. A boy should never kiss a girl without permission. It isn't right."

Amy looked thoughtful for a minute. "Then you better ask next time. Or Mommy will wash your mouth out with soap or give you a time out." She nodded sagely.

"Good advice. I'll remember that. I apologize, Lisa. It won't happen again. Without permission." He turned his head so Amy couldn't see and winked at Lisa.

"Apology accepted. Come on, Amy. It's time to get home and cleaned up and have a snack. I made cookies last night."

"Can Mr. Cam come?"

"I haven't had home-baked cookies in ages."

"Seriously?" He was pulling the pity card? Low. Very low.

"Mom, we better give him cookies, 'cause nobody bakes for him."

Good gravy. Why was the kindness and generosity she tried to teach Amy coming back to bite her on the butt? There was no way to win this argument.

"Fine." She heard the grudging agreement in her voice but couldn't muster up the strength to care about being uncharitable.

"Yay," the dynamic duo whooped in unison.

"Come on, Amy. Let's pick up these toys before Mom changes her mind." They raced back to the sandbox and gathered the toys in record time. "If it's okay with your mom, you can keep the sand toys."

Amy looked at Lisa for approval.

"You can keep them. Say thank you."

"Thanks. I loves them." Amy smiled at him. "Come on, Mom." She took Cam's hand, and they skipped away, headed for home.

He skipped? Who was this man, and what had he done with the devil-may-care bachelor she'd known only days ago? Today, he seemed too much like a family man. This wasn't good. How was she supposed to resist him like this?

As she followed them home, half her time was lost in thought. The other half was spent admiring his butt. He did have one glorious backside.

CHAPTER 19

A few nights later, Cam stood on the sidewalk in front of Lisa's place. The bright green house had white shutters and was surrounded by fall flowers. She must cover them at night. It was getting cold in the evenings now, and the likelihood of frost at this elevation was high.

He was as nervous as hell. He'd dressed up for this. Clean, pressed jeans. A button-down shirt, with the sleeves rolled up to his forearms. He'd showered and shaved. And he wasn't sure he should be here. She'd never actually retracted her invitation to dinner, but she hadn't reissued it either. This could go very badly.

Opening the passenger door of his truck, he extracted a bouquet of flowers and a shopping bag.

"Well, here goes nothing." He strode up the walk and tapped on the front door.

He heard Amy's chatter overtop the sound of the television. Footsteps clicked toward the door. He held his breath until it opened. Lisa wore an uncertain smile and the hottest dress he'd ever seen.

"Hi." He swallowed hard. The dress was bright yellow with some kind of flower print on it. It was short and tight and showed off Lisa's long legs to drooling advantage. She wore short, spiky heels which accentuated those legs and made him drool. He couldn't stop his gaze from traveling from the tip of her open-toed shoes to the hem of the dress. She looked incredible. Perfect. And way too good for him.

"Hi, Cam. I wasn't sure you'd show up."

"Am I still invited?" He offered her the flowers.

"I'll be honest. I waffled. I debated not cooking. I thought about not being home when you got here. And about a thousand other means of escape."

He winced. "Ouch. I guess I deserve that." He held out the shopping bag. "Here. I brought a bottle of wine to go with dinner and a book for Amy. I'll go now."

She reached out, not for the bag, but to place her hand on his arm. The light contact scalded enough he almost jerked his arm away.

"Stay. You've been good to us. You helped us out of a tight spot. The least I can do is repay you with dinner."

"You don't owe me anything. Is this a gratitude dinner?"

"Yes. No."

She huffed out a tortured sigh.

"I mean, I don't know what this is." She took the bag and waved him inside. "Come on. Dinner will be ready in a few minutes."

"Are you sure?" He hated the hesitance in his voice.

She laughed at the question.

"You know what? I'm not sure. Not about dinner. Not about you. Not about anything. You rattle me. I don't know what to make of you, and it scares me."

He stared at her. Her smile was wobbly and uncertain. "I'll just go then. I don't want to make you uncomfortable. Enjoy the wine. Say hi to Amy for me." He turned to go.

"Wait!"

The volume of her voice startled him, and he jerked back around.

"Stay. Please."

"I don't think that's for the best." His stomach clenched uncomfortably. Good grief. There was nothing he wanted more than to be with her, and here he was offering to leave? What was up in his head?

"See, that's what I mean."

"What?" He gawked at her.

"One minute, I think you're the consummate bachelor then you turn around and act like a real man. Caring. Respectful. I don't get it." Her brows pinched together.

"Me, either." He chuckled at his own ineptness. "Sometimes, I feel bipolar. You know, changing directions like the wind. You confuse me. I'm not looking for long term, and I know it's what you want. It's what you need. But the truth is, I don't do long term, but for the life of me, I can't stay away. I like you, and I like your daughter."

"Then join us for dinner. Please."

She sounded sincere, as if she actually wanted him there. It didn't make any sense. She should be chasing him off. And he should be running away as far and as fast as he could. He hesitated, frozen between entering and turning tail and bolting. She deserved better than him.

Still, he stepped inside. The aroma of roast beef caressed his nose, and he inhaled deeply. Mmm. Gravy and potatoes and, unless he missed his guess, carrots.

"Wow. That smells heavenly."

"Roast beef and Yorkshire pudding as promised. And better than your sister makes, too."

"I highly doubt that. Her recipe's been in the family for years, though my mom couldn't cook to save her life."

"Does she like cooking?"

"I've never asked her. We don't talk much. But she never seemed to like it."

"You don't talk to your parents? Why on earth not?"

"Dad's gone. As for Mom… My childhood wasn't the best. They fought all the time. Mom rarely ever cooked. She was always off at some book club meeting or out for drinks with the girls. We ate a lot of pancakes and macaroni. But my grandmother could cook like nobody's business. She taught Ang everything she knows. Ang can kick any master chef's ass in the kitchen." He laughed. "But don't ever tell her I told you so."

"Siblings." Lisa laughed, too. "I hear they're a pain. I always wanted a sister."

"I didn't know you were an only child." Somehow, that surprised him. She had the air of someone who had a huge family, as if she loved big.

He tried not to leer at her legs and backside as he followed her past a small but functional living room into the kitchen. In bright and sunny colors, it had a huge window, open to catch the early evening breeze. Through it, he saw the backyard, including several large trees and a swing set.

"I am. And I never intended for Amy to be an only child, but life has a way of changing a person's plans. Davin died way too early, but I'm blessed to have Amy." She shrugged eloquently. "I guess I'm still hoping to find Mr. Right and have more children. I love kids. I want a bushel of them."

"I'll consider myself warned." Funny, the idea of having children didn't freak him out, right now. Not here, in this room with Lisa anyway.

"I didn't mean it like that."

"I know you didn't. You've been clear you're looking for long term; I'm looking for short term. But I think, despite that, we can be friends."

She studied him up and down, making him wonder what she

was thinking. A small smile curled up the corner of her mouth. Whatever she had on her mind seemed to be good. He'd take that.

"Cam! You're here." Amy skidded into the kitchen, her socks sliding on the spotless floor. "Come play with me."

"Hi, Amy. I brought you a book." He looked at Lisa who handed him the book.

"Yay! I love books. Can you read it to me?" She hopped up and down excitedly.

"If it's okay with your mom."

"Please, Mommy." She drew both words out longingly, making Cam laugh.

"I don't mind if Mr. Cam doesn't. Then you have to wash up for dinner."

"Come on, Kiddo. Let's read."

Dancing with excitement, Amy led him into the living room. He had only a moment to look around before she practically dragged him to an easy chair in the corner. The room was pinpoint neat, even if the furniture was well-worn. There was an overflowing bookcase in the corner, the bottom shelves filled with children's books, the upper shelves full of novels and what looked to be textbooks. Another corner held a heaping toy box of well-loved toys. A puzzle was started on the table in the adjacent dining room. Colorful children's paintings, no doubt created by Amy, adorned the walls. More than anything else, the room looked like love.

"This is the bestest reading chair."

He settled into the easy chair, and she climbed right into his lap, handing him the book. She wiggled and shifted until she was nestled into his side, his arm around her waist. He opened the book and started to read.

When he finished the book, he looked up to find Lisa leaning against the doorjamb looking at them with a bittersweet smile. "Dinner's ready. Amy, go wash up."

Amy scampered down and disappeared down the hall.

"That's a sad smile." He crossed the room and caressed her cheek.

"A bit."

He didn't speak. He wanted to know but was pretty sure she didn't want to share the reason for the sadness in her eyes.

"That was my husband's chair. He never got to read to Amy. He died when she was barely two, hardly more than an infant."

"I'm so sorry." He swallowed hard. "I didn't mean to impose." He floundered for a moment, looking for the right words.

"It's okay. She loved reading with you. I'm glad you took the time. He would be, too."

"Thanks. I enjoyed it. I love reading to my sister's kids." And he did. There was something touching about having a child on your lap. The cuddles were nice, and their rapt attention was special. Even when they were only half-paying attention he liked reading to little ones. But that didn't mean he wanted one of his own.

"I appreciate you inviting me to dinner."

"Call it a thank you for helping us out." She waved for him to follow her into the kitchen.

In the short time he'd taken to read to Amy, she'd set the table and had the food dished up. Impressive. The roast beef steamed on a platter beside a bowl of mashed potatoes. There were carrots, gravy, salad and Yorkshire pudding. This might be the best meal he'd had in months, if not longer.

"Wow. It looks and smells fabulous."

"Would you like to carve the meat?" She gestured to the large knife and carving fork beside the platter. "Afterward, I'll put the knife away, out of Amy's reach."

"I'd be happy to."

Amy slid into the room and climbed up to the table as he sliced the beef.

"Careful, Munchkin. Sharp knives can be dangerous."

"Yes, sir."

She sat quietly while he carved. Lisa poured milk for Amy and wine for the adults. She settled in her chair and said, "Let's say grace. Would you like to say it, Cam?"

Oh crap. He hadn't been expecting that. It wasn't he didn't believe in God. It was more that he didn't actively participate in his belief. Nothing like being put on the spot. *Think man, think.*

Out of nowhere came a blessing from his childhood.

"Bless us, oh Lord, for these gifts which we are about to receive, through Thy bounty, through Christ our Lord we pray. Amen."

"Amen. That was a nice blessing. Simple and thoughtful. I didn't know you were religious."

"Um. I'm not exactly. But I'm not *not* religious either." He stumbled over the words to express his views. "I mean, I believe in God, most of the time. But I don't go to church or practice organized religion in any fashion."

"Many people don't. It isn't the religion that's important. It's the belief."

Her soft smile made his heart pound. Good grief. Was her approval important to him?

"Why only most of the time?" She drove right to the point.

"That's a tough one." He thought about it for a moment, trying to organize his feelings on the delicate subject. "Sometimes, when good things go bad or bad things happen to good people, I wonder why it has to be like that."

"It's about balance." She made a leveling motion with her hands, similar to a balance scale. "Think of it this way. I love pizza. I mean I totally adore pizza. I could eat it every day for the rest of my life. But I'm pretty sure, after a while, it would get old. So, if I broke up the continual diet of pizza with a salad, salad would seem pretty spectacular. You need the bad to balance the good. Without the bad for perspective, the good has no meaning. It all becomes the same."

"My grandmother said something like that once. I was about ten, I guess. We were watching the news, and I thought it was tragic when someone got killed. We watched the article and saw all the flowers and gifts left at the scene of the accident. She reminded me that, while the deaths were tragic, for the people selling the flowers, it was a helpful thing. She didn't mean it was good to profit from the loss of others. She meant the bad had a good side, a silver lining. She always told me to look for the good in everything bad. It isn't easy when something goes tragically wrong though."

"Like when your father died? That must have been painful for you."

"It was. And it wasn't. He was my dad. I loved him. But he was a mean drunk and always fighting with my mother. It was a relief when her suffering ended." He focused on eating for a few bites, hoping she'd drop the subject. His grandmother had always said you never discuss religion or politics at the table. When he looked up, Lisa looked thoughtful and Amy disgruntled.

"Sorry, Amy. I forgot you were here. How was daycare today?"

"Good. We played parachute!"

"Parachute?" He glanced at Lisa for clarification. She laughed.

"They have a big, circular piece of cloth, like a parachute. They wave it up and down, play under it, run around it...the usual kid games."

"Wow, that sounds like fun."

"It's my favorite. I love it best." She smiled broadly and rambled on about the games. The rest of dinner revolved around her friends and daycare.

Cam helped Lisa clear the table and wash up the dishes. Amy cleared her own place then ran off to watch her half hour of television before bed.

"Dinner was great. Thank you."

"Better than your sister's?"

"Fishing for compliments?" he teased.

"Dang right."

"Okay, I admit it. It was better than Ang makes, but if you tell her, I'll deny it."

"Cross my heart. Should I ever meet your paragon of a sister, I shall never divulge your dark secret." She laughed.

"Careful there. I'll hold you to that." He chuckled and hung up his dish towel.

"Coffee?"

"Yes, please. Unless you want me to go. You probably have a bedtime ritual with Amy."

"I do, but if you don't mind waiting a bit, I'll put coffee on, and we'll share a cup after she's down. It won't take long."

"I'm in."

"Decaf?"

"Never!" He feigned horror.

"A man after my own heart. It's high-test all the way for this girl."

A short time later, they sat together on the couch. Close, but not quite touching. She'd poured a touch of coffee liqueur into each glass. It was smooth and delicious, with just a hint of chocolate.

"This is nice." He winced inwardly at his inane comment.

"It is. I'm glad you came. I'm enjoying myself." She smiled broadly, kicked off her heels and pivoted on the couch, tossing her legs over his lap. Her feet rested on one side of him, her butt on the other. But in between, she barely touched him. It was purely innocent, and at the same time, as sexy and as enticing as hell. Surprised, he stiffened beneath her. She put her feet on the floor.

"Sorry. I didn't mean to presume," she apologized.

"Presume?" He laughed and edged her legs back where they had been. "I just wasn't expecting it."

"What were you expecting?"

"Well…"

He heard the hesitation in her voice. He'd better tread lightly. "You're confusing sometimes. Hot one minute; cold the next."

She jerked her legs back and glared.

"Wait." He made a hold-it motion with his hands. "I get it. I'm not what you're looking for, but you're attracted to me despite that.

You don't know how to handle it. Frankly, I don't either. You're smart and funny. Sexy as hell. Sometimes, you take my breath away."

She laughed. "Yeah, right."

"Seriously. I've never met anyone like you. I want you. I need you. But…"

"But…there ain't no way you're ever gonna love me? Classic rock lyrics? Really?"

"No. Yes. Fuck. I don't know."

Her angry response worried him. His thighs tensed, and he fidgeted on the couch.

"I can't help how I feel any more than you can," he admitted.

She jerked to her feet, slamming her cup down on the coffee table. "I think you better go."

The tension in her arms and quaver in her voice warned of an impending explosion. Shit.

He set his cup beside hers, stood and placed his hands on her shoulders. "Look, I've been up front with my feelings and the way I do things from the beginning. I've never led you astray or lied to you. We don't want the same things. But I think we can work something out." There had to be a way to remain friends.

"Something?" she screeched. "What? You want me to be your dirty little secret? You could swing by when it's convenient and do me before you walk away?"

He winced. He should have known this was coming. The past had shown him time and time again. His mother, his ex… Women had a tendency to read what they wanted into a man's words then be offended when they didn't get what they wanted. It was why he never dated women who didn't share his agenda.

"I didn't mean it like that."

"Shut up." She lurched out of his grasp. "Shut up and get the hell out of my house."

"Lisa. Please."

"Go! Now! Stay away from me and my daughter."

He raised his hands in supplication. "Okay. I'll go. But I didn't mean to hurt you. I meant to…"

"Meant to what? Screw me? Screw with my head? Get me into your bed by using my daughter to soften me up? Grow up, Cam. Grow some balls. Man up. You're way too old to be tomcatting around. Show some respect for women."

"I'll have you know I'm still friends with every woman I've ever dated. Well, except one and she doesn't count."

"Is she the one who damaged you?" Her voice was hard and unforgiving.

"I. Am. Not. Damaged." His voice rose with each word. "I'm a man. I like women. Women like me. If I don't want something permanent, there's no shame in it. And I'd never use a child like that."

"Get out." She stabbed one finger toward the door. "Go!"

"What's the sense in arguing with a woman? You're all irrational."

THROUGH THE LIVING ROOM WINDOW, Lisa watched him walk away. He paused beside his truck, looking back at the house. She wrapped her arms around herself and stepped back out of view. No sense letting him see how badly he'd upset her. She'd be damned if she'd give him the satisfaction.

She'd been right about him from the start. Sure, he was nice enough, but he was way too much playboy for the likes of her. She needed mature and stable, not hump everything that moves. She knew better than to discount her gut feelings. She was good at reading people, and he'd stunk of "fling" from the very start. Well, she was done with him now. He could stay away from her and her daughter. She wanted nothing to do with him. She was too good for a one-timer like Cam.

So why did his words hurt so badly?

She wiped a tear off her cheek.

Nope.

No way.

She wouldn't cry over him. Not today. Not ever. There were other good men out there. She'd find the right one eventually. It didn't have to be Mr. Too-Sexy-For-His-Own-Good. There were other eligible bachelors in Haven. Like Nick. She laughed at the thought. Nick was great. Handsome, witty, charming. But he definitely didn't ring her bell or set her heart on fire. Her friendship with Nick would never be more than that.

But Cam had shown up in town, so there was hope someone else would, too.

She'd just box up her emotions and set them aside. Then she'd wait. Heaven had a plan for her; she was sure of it. She just had to be patient.

She wandered around the house, picking up their mugs and tidying throw pillows. He left her so disconcerted. As if she'd lost something she hadn't even known she wanted. He was messing with her head. Probably not on purpose. It was just who he was. Fun and games. He wasn't her type, but she wanted to get to know him better, and that would likely lead to her getting hurt.

"Yeah, because I'm not hurt already." She flopped down onto the couch. It was times like this she wondered what God's plan for her was. Was she destined to be alone for the rest of her life? Or was there something better in store for her? If she could just break through Cam's wall, make him see relationships were a good thing...

"Don't go there," she warned herself. "People don't change. You know that." She picked up the television remote and flicked through the channels. News. Reality TV. Game shows. Romantic comedy. She kept flicking. Live comedians. She needed a few good laughs for distraction. She settled in to watch but missed a lot of jokes because she couldn't concentrate.

CHAPTER 20

Lisa, Natalie and Grace sat in the church basement, chugging coffee and working on their plans for the Christmas carnival. A lot of the work was already done, and now, they were getting down to the nitty-gritty. With only a week until the carnival, time was running out.

"You want me to work with who?" Lisa stared at Grace.

"Cam." Grace laughed.

"I don't think so. Nope. I'm out." She folded her arms over her chest belligerently. She knew she was being unreasonable, but she was still irked at him. She'd avoided him since their disastrous argument six weeks ago, and she'd continue to ignore him until he left town.

"Why not? It's for a good cause."

"Because he's a colossal turd."

"A turd. Wow. Harsh words." Natalie's eyes twinkled with laughter. "Admit it; you like him."

Why couldn't they just let it go? Why did friends have to push?

"You know we love you, right?" Grace asked.

"Get out of my head." Lisa laughed. "It's like you're reading my mind. You're freaking me out."

"I…have a gift for reading your mind." Grace shuffled some papers on the table. "That's what good friends do, plus they nag each other. Cam's a good guy, but his home life sucked. His parents had a terrible marriage. Sterling told me how Cam's ex-fiancée hurt him pretty badly. But he likes you. A lot. I think you should give him a chance."

"That's just it. I do like him, but I can't give him a chance. Amy could get attached to him. She'd be devastated if he went away. And he will. He's only here temporarily."

"He's portable," Natalie added.

"Portable? What do you mean?"

"Portable: able to move. Not fixed in one place. He could move here. He *is* Sterling's partner, and they're moving the main office here. Or you could move to the city. Don't limit yourself based on geography. Don't run away from something that could be good."

"I'm not running from anything. We hardly know each other. We've had one dinner together and gone to the park with Amy. There's nothing to run from."

"I notice you left out the fact you lived with him after your neighbors' house burned down," Natalie teased.

"Irrelevant. That was forced circumstances. I shared a room with him. I did not live with him. Besides, there's nothing between us."

"How about attraction?" It was Grace's turn to play devil's advocate.

"I'm not attracted to him." Lisa looked away, unable to face her friend when telling an outright lie. Guilt rode her. "Okay, I'm attracted to him, but he's not for me. I'm not sure he's for anyone."

"Think about it," Natalie advised. "I have to run and pick up Mathew."

"See you tomorrow," Lisa and Grace replied in unison. Natalie gave them a finger wave then disappeared out the door.

"You surprise me," Grace said. "You always talk about how good marriage with Davin was. He was your childhood sweetheart, and you lost him. You know how much losing love sucks. I've been there, so I know. Take a chance. Date him. Maybe not formally but give him a chance to realize what you have to offer. Take a risk. Love is worth it. You know it as well as I do."

"I can't risk it. Just drop the subject, Grace. Let it go."

"Will you at least work with him for the Christmas carnival? We need his construction skills for props and sets for the Nativity play and concert. I've already asked for his help. He's precutting simple Nativity stables for the kids to assemble as crafts. And we need your help with the kids. You're great with them, and he's great with wood. It's like a match made in heaven. Don't make me pull out the pity card. Please." She batted her eyes furiously, and they both laughed.

"Fine."

"Excellent," Cam said from the doorway behind them.

Turning toward the door, Lisa took him in from the top of his perfectly groomed hair to the tips of his casual shoes. Neat jeans, a button-down shirt and freshly shaved, he sure cleaned up well. He was a sight for a lonely woman's eyes.

Her pulse surged. Darn, he was good-looking. No, that didn't quite cover it. He wasn't handsome in a pretty way, more in a clean-cut but still rugged fashion. Even in December, he had a hint of a tan, and those long eyelashes… Wow. Swoon-worthy.

"Do you eavesdrop everywhere you go?" Lisa snapped to cover her attraction.

"Nope. Only where I might overhear something interesting." He strolled up to them. Spinning a chair around, he sat with his arms crossed on its back.

"How long were you listening?" Damn him. How much had he heard? Hopefully, not too much. The last thing she needed was him knowing she was still attracted to him.

"Long enough." He winked.

Jeepers. She just couldn't catch a break. It was bad enough she couldn't stop thinking about him. Now, she had to work with him, and he might know she liked him. Crap. Crap. Crap.

"So, how's this going to work. What will I have to do?" Lisa asked, ignoring Cam and turning toward Grace.

"I've got the prototype here." He swung a backpack off his shoulder and rummaged inside. He set a small, simply constructed wooden building on the table. "It finishes like this." He dug in the bag again. "I've made bases with grooves. Three walls will be glued into the slots and to each other. Then we'll glue two roof pieces to the top. They're grooved, too." He flipped the roof pieces over and traced the indentations with his fingers. "It's all basic, groove-and-glue construction. Add a bit of hay, or something, to the floor, and there you have it. A three-sided building with a peaked roof suitable for housing the Holy Family."

"That's ingenious." Lisa smiled despite herself. "Quick, easy and foolproof. What were you thinking for the floor?"

"Well, it's a barn. So, maybe, some actual hay?" He shrugged.

"What about raffia?" Grace suggested.

"Raffia?" Cam looked puzzled.

"It's a stringy, crafty supply which looks like grass. It's made from palm trees, I think. There's some here." Moving across the room, Grace rummaged in a cupboard brimming with craft supplies then came back, brandishing a handful of raffia strands. "It'll glue in easily, and it's pretty durable. That'll cut down on the mess."

"Grace, you're brilliant. I'll cut it into pieces that'll fit well." Lisa turned to Cam. "Is this the final size?"

"It is. What about people? Doesn't the Nativity need people and animals?"

"That's another craft station. The kids will move from station to station. By the end of the afternoon, they'll have a complete Nativity scene to take home. Then there's cookies and juice. We'll have some games, too. Why are you doing this?" Lisa blurted. "You don't believe in God."

"I didn't say that. I said I sometimes question my belief and His motives."

"Let's not turn this into an argument, guys. Let's just work together. I've lined up a couple teenagers to help. They'll run errands and babysit some of the younger kids, which lets the adults enjoy themselves, too." Grace looked back and forth between them, clearly hoping the argument was over. "I'll be reading Christmas books, both religious and secular. That's why I need you guys to run this part of the craft."

"Is this a fundraiser or what?" Cam asked.

"Yes and no. We won't deny anyone admission. We're asking for cash donations for the church, the food bank and the toy drive. But it's all voluntary. It's about sharing and giving and the miracle of Christmas."

"I love Christmas." Lisa sighed. "So much joy and hope. It's probably my favorite time of year."

"Except for Valentine's Day," Grace injected. "All that chocolate, all those treats."

Lisa sighed. "Chocolate. Mmm." She shook her head to clear the delectable idea of chocolate's sweet bliss. "Is there anything you need me to do to help with the kits? We'll probably need about a hundred and fifty of them. We get in a lot of town folk for the carnival. It isn't just the usual congregation."

"A hundred and fifty? Shit." His cheeks turned red. "I better get busy. And sorry for swearing in church."

"Technically, we aren't in church. We're in the basement. But apology accepted." Lisa smiled at him. "Can you be here early on Saturday, the twenty-second? About nine. That'll give us time to finish setting up. I'll bring coffee and donuts. Lunch is on the church."

"I can do that. See you Saturday." He stood and repacked his bag. "Catch you then." He kissed the top of her head then disappeared out the door.

"Wow." Grace stared after him. "He's got it bad."

"What?" Lisa turned to her friend. "What did you say? I wasn't listening."

"No, you were staring at his ass." She chuckled. "He's got it bad, and you do, too. You guys are meant to be together."

"And you're exaggerating."

"Am not."

"Are too."

They dissolved into laughter. It was a long while before they settled enough to finish the carnival plans.

AMY WAS BEYOND EXHAUSTED. She'd reached the break-into-tears-at-drop-of-a-hat phase. She'd missed her nap and wanted to cling to Lisa. When she wasn't asking for cuddles, she clamored to know if Santa would bring her a kitten. Cam had taken her aside to guide her in the craft. Within a few moments, he had her laughing and giggling. Her stable was together—a bit lopsided, but together.

"Here, hold it like this." Cam demonstrated how to dip the bottom of one wall into the glue and settle it in the groove of the base. "You have to hold it still. Count to twenty. Count with me, Amy. One, two, three…"

Amy joined him in counting, floundering occasionally and stumbling on the teens. When the piece had dried enough, he helped her with the second wall. Lisa watched with a smile. He was patient.

They'd been at this for most of the day. Now, the crowd had dwindled to almost nothing. Cam seemed to have a knack to coaching several children at once. He'd managed to keep a tight rein on the rowdy ones without dampening their spirits. He drew the quiet and shy ones out equally as well. It fascinated her to watch him interact with them. He seemed to have an instinct for knowing how to handle each child.

"You're good with kids."

"I'm doing okay." He looked away.

"Actually, you're excellent. I would have strangled more than a couple of those beasts. I swear some of their parents left them here alone."

"Who would do that to their kids?" He sounded upset.

"Okay, they probably didn't, but six hours of this is way too long for this girl. We should have split this into shifts." She straightened a pile of raffia and wiped up some glue drops as she talked. "And it's a good thing you thought to cover the table in plastic. Cleanup will be a breeze."

"That's a good thing since you've been wiping glue off the floor all day. You know what? You deserve a break. How about if I take you and Amy out for D.I.N.N.E.R? Not a date. Just exhausted friends eating together."

"We're gonna eat together?" Amy chimed in excitedly.

"She can spell?" He sounded incredulous. Lisa laughed.

"No, goofball. You said eating together. A baby could catch that."

"And here I tried to spell in case you didn't want to join me." He looked away, making her wonder what he was hiding.

"I appreciate the gesture. Kids never miss a trick, though. And yes, we'd like to join you for dinner. But if you don't mind, can we have takeout at my place? Amy is exhausted, and I'm worried she'll be difficult. Four-year-olds don't have the greatest self-control." She smiled fondly at her daughter. "I love her to bits, but I know her limits. Nobody needs to be subjected to a cranky child during their dinner."

He ruffled Amy's hair. "She's pretty awesome, but I can see she's tired. Takeout it is. Any preferences? Sid's? Pizza?"

"Chinese? There's a new Chinese place. I hear they've got great food. Lemon chicken would be fabulous." Her stomach growled. "I'm starving."

"Chinese, it is. Any requests, besides lemon chicken? Any no-nos?"

"I'm pretty flexible. I'll eat almost anything. Can you grab some plain rice, please? Amy won't eat fried rice. It'll take me about forty-five minutes to finish up here. Do you want to grab the food and meet at my place in about an hour?"

~

A SOFT KNOCK on the front door alerted her to Cam's arrival. She hopped up and scurried to the door. Pausing, she smoothed her sweater and jeans, pasted a smile on her face then opened the door.

"Hi. Come in."

He stepped inside, handed her the bag and shucked his coat. Draping it on a hook in the corner, he smiled warmly at her. "Hi. Where's the munchkin?"

"In bed. She fell asleep on the couch, so I put her to bed. She's had a long day."

"Won't she get hungry?"

"Probably. If she wakes up, I'll feed her." She shrugged. "Let's eat. I'm starving. Unless you object, we'll eat out here." She led him to the living room and placed the takeout bag on a tray on the coffee table. Flopping down on a throw pillow on the floor, she smiled up at him. "Pull up a stump."

"Sure thing. I'm starved." He opened the bag and extracted the boxes, reciting their contents as he went. "Ginger beef, special fried rice, plain rice, lemon chicken, beef spring rolls, chicken Chow Mein, beef and greens, and last but not least, garlic dry ribs."

She laughed. "How many people did you think you were feeding?"

"Come on. I spent the entire day with a roomful of rugrats, and I do physical work all day. I have a big appetite." He winked.

Jeepers. Making the simplest response into an innuendo was so easy for him. She turned away, so he didn't see her blush. "It looks delicious. What do I owe you?"

"Nothing. My treat. You worked hard today."

"So did you. You were great with the kids." She grabbed a spoon and started piling food on her plate.

"It was more fun than I'd expected," he confessed.

"If you didn't think you'd enjoy it, why did you agree to help out?" She pinned him with a glance.

He didn't say anything until he'd loaded his plate with food. "Honestly? I don't know. Guilt? Because Grace pressured me into it? Wanting to help the community? I like Haven. Wanting to be near you and the munchkin? Christmas spirit?" He ate a couple mouthfuls. "The truth is I don't know why. But it was better than I'd expected and worse. But I'm glad I went."

"I know what you mean. Some of those kids can drive you crazy in three seconds. But I love kids, and I like helping the community. We collected fifty boxes of food for the Christmas baskets. I don't know what we raised for the church, but it will go toward toys for underprivileged kids and to round out the food baskets. I'm thrilled with our success."

"Excellent. No kid should have a crappy Christmas because their parents are having tough times." He turned his attention to his food.

"You say that like you've lived it. Not meaning to pry, of course."

"We never hurt for money, and we always had enough to eat, even if it wasn't the best or most nutritious food."

Lisa studied his profile. He looked tense. She waited for more but braced herself for letting the subject drop.

"I had a friend in grade school. He didn't have a father, and his mother worked triple shifts some days. She worked every holiday. His Christmases always sucked. One year, I gave him the handheld gaming system I'd gotten from Santa. He was so thrilled someone remembered him. But man, my dad was pissed. He spanked me. Hard. Too hard. I had bruises for a week. But you know what? The pleasure on Tim's face was worth it."

"That was so generous of you. Especially since your father over-reacted."

"He did overreact, it was his go-to move. Everything was always a crisis. Especially when he was drunk. That's why I give money to the food bank and toy drives every year. No kid deserves crappy holidays."

She placed her hand on his forearm. "That's very kind of you. I'll bet Tim remembers you, even now. And all those other children appreciate it." She studied him, noticing the blush which crept up his face. She'd embarrassed him. "You're a good man, Cameron Zeus."

She dropped her hand and resumed eating.

LISA'S PRAISE made him uncomfortable. Cam hadn't done anything special. Not then and not today. He looked away, avoiding her knowing look. He noticed her Christmas decorations for the first time.

Her living room looked like a department store Christmas display. Every flat surface was adorned with something holiday related. Amy's Nativity scene and another one graced an end table. There was a snowman quilt on the back of the couch. Red and green candles and bunches of pine and greenery were everywhere. He took a deep breath. Cedar, cranberry, pine and cinnamon filled his nose. Memories of holidays with his grandmother rushed in. Those had been good times. Happiness, love and laughter in a tiny house brimming with love.

Just like during his childhood with his grandmother, Lisa had a huge, live tree filled one corner, and lights and ornaments decorated it to within an inch of its life. Many were store-bought, some looked antique, but a lot of them were poorly crafted ornaments which hung alongside the others, a sure sign of a proud mother.

"Wow. I just noticed the decorations." He gestured widely with one hand. "I guess Amy made a lot of them. I like the one-eyed reindeer." He pointed to a lopsided reindeer made from wooden spoons. It had mangled antlers and only one eye. Half of its pompom nose was missing.

"She made that at daycare last year. She was so proud of it, though I doubt she'll feel the same when she's a teenager."

"I'll bet, when she's a teenager, she'll love the fact you love her enough to display all her projects with such pride."

"You think so?"

"I know so. My grandmother still shows off the lopsided vase I made in kindergarten. It's the ugliest damn thing I've ever seen, but she still uses it. Part of me wishes she'd just throw it away. I've given her a crystal one to replace it, but she says you can't replace love with glass."

"That's so sweet. She's right, you know? There's something extra special about a gift crafted with love."

"Even if it's ugly? Because that vase was danged ugly." He laughed.

"I think that's the point. You cared enough to make it; which makes it priceless. It's like Amy's reindeer or her lopsided Nativity. I'll always treasure them because she made them for me. Nothing, not even a Faberge Nativity, is as valuable."

"Faberge makes Nativities?" He winked at her.

She mock-slapped his arm. "You know what I mean."

"I do. I just hadn't thought of it like that."

They talked and ate until they were both stuffed. Their conversation wasn't anything important, except it allowed them time to get to know one another better. Eventually, he knew it was time to go. He stood and stacked their dishes then carried them to the kitchen. He rinsed the plates and loaded them in the dishwasher while she packed up the leftovers.

"Take this with you." She held out the bag.

"I can't. I don't have a fridge at Harmony's. Besides, I'm going to see my grandmother for Christmas. I'll be gone several days. You keep them." He took the bag from her and slid it into the refrigerator.

"Thank you. For the leftovers, for helping at the carnival, and for a lovely evening." Her smile was soft and gracious.

"Thank you. I enjoyed myself. It's been a good day."

At the front door, he slid into his coat and boots. He stood there a moment, looking at her. Dang, she was beautiful. Inside and out. He leaned forward and kissed her softly on the cheek. "Goodnight, sweet Lisa. I'll miss you. I'll be back in a few days. I'd like to see you again."

"Goodbye, Cam. Drive safe. See you when you get back."

As he walked to the truck, he realized her statement had been a general one, not a promise. He was disappointed but understood her reasoning. As attracted as they were to each other, he didn't still want anything long term. Their needs were different, and he had to respect that. He didn't like it, but he respected it.

He sat in the truck, staring at the house until all the lights were out. Then reluctantly, he pulled away and headed for the bed and breakfast.

CHAPTER 21

Christmas came and went. And New Year's Eve did, too. Lisa didn't fret about being alone for the holidays. At least, not too much. Holidays had always been spent with Davin from the year she'd met him until his death. Now, she spent them with Amy. In the past, Clint had come for Christmas dinner, and they'd spent New Year's laughing over old, silent movies. This year, they'd had Christmas dinner with Clint and his new wife, Natalie. Amy had enjoyed playing with their son, Mathew.

New Year's Eve had been a quiet evening alone at home with Amy.

Clint had closed the café for New Year's Day, and now, it was the second day of January and routine knocked on her door again.

Outside, she heard the continual beep-beep of trucks and equipment backing up. Generators and air compressors added a deafening din to the morning. The noise was exacerbated by the continual whine of power saws and the thump-thumping of air-nailers. She didn't have to look outside to know reconstruction had begun on the neighbors' house.

She hadn't expected it to start until spring, but it appeared she'd been wrong.

Bundled up and ready for the short walk to daycare, Lisa and Amy headed out the door. The cacophony of construction was deafening. If this kept up, they'd need earplugs inside the house. Yikes, she'd forgotten how loud building a house got.

"There's Mr. Cam!" Amy shouted and waved frantically.

Cam jogged over to them. His hard hat and well-worn jeans gave him a rough-and-tumble appeal that took her breath away.

"Hey, Pixie-Sticks. Sorry about the racket." He skipped a normal greeting. "We'll be pouring concrete late today, as soon as the forms are finished. Then we'll erect a plastic dome to trap the heat. Then the noise will drop, except for the generators and heaters. We need to keep it above freezing in the dome, so the concrete will set properly. Today should be the only day we work extra late. We'll probably be banging around until late evening. I hope that's okay."

"Late evening? That's a long day for you." Lisa sighed silently. Getting Amy to bed would be an issue. Just what she needed, an overtired kid unable to sleep.

"It's just this one night." His smile was hopeful. "Most days, we'll quit around six, but it's best if we can get the concrete done in a day. I know it'll be a huge pain for you, but we don't have much choice if we want to get this thing built."

"We'll survive one night. I'll just have to figure out how to turn this into an adventure. I'm glad the Restinols will have their house back soon."

"Well, not soon exactly. But sooner than if we waited until spring to get started. All the paperwork's in place. We're double shifting where we can to get it done earlier. We're hoping for a mid-April completion."

"It takes that long to build a house? I had no idea." She laughed at her naivety. "I never really thought about it. When I was a kid, it seemed like new neighborhoods went up overnight."

"Not so much. After the basement, we finish the exterior. Then it quiets down for the neighbors. It won't be silent but working inside is less disruptive for you. And except for today, I'll make sure the exterior crews finish up before Amy's bedtime."

"Thank you." It was considerate of him to think of them and the other neighbors with small children. "I appreciate your concern."

A warm smile crept over his face, sending tingles all the way to her toes.

"You could repay me with dinner some night?" His words were both a statement and a question.

She tapped one gloved finger on her lips. "Perhaps. I shall consider your request and get back to you."

"I'll give you my cell number."

She laughed. "I'm pretty sure I know where to find you."

He laughed along with her. Dang, she loved a guy with a sense of humor.

He knelt in front of Amy. "How was your Christmas? Was Santa good to you?"

"He brought me a toboggan and skates and a board game and some number cards and Legos."

"Wow, that's quite a haul." He gently interrupted what looked to be a lengthy list. "You must have been very good to get so many presents."

"Mommy says I was extra special before Christmas. But today, I was bad when I broke the toilet." She hung her head.

He looked up at Lisa, questions in his eyes.

"She flushed half a roll of paper towel this morning. It's plugged solid, and my plunger doesn't work for crap."

He groaned. "You had to go there?"

"Sorry, I can't resist a crappy pun." She chuckled at her bad joke.

"Tell you what, Amy. I'll stop by after work, and you and I can fix that nasty toilet together."

"Yay!"

"You don't need to do that."

Their words collided midsentence.

"I know, but I'm pretty good with toilets." He puffed up his shoulders and looked all serious. "I can unclog the best of them."

"What about work? I thought you were working late?"

"I can spare the ten minutes it takes to unclog a toilet. Then you can repay me with a late dinner." His grin was roguish and unrepentant.

"I can, can I?" She should be annoyed with his pushiness, but strangely, she wasn't.

"I'd appreciate it. Honestly, by the time we're finished and I shower, there won't be anything open but the pub, and I'm about filled up with pub food. I'd kill for a home-cooked meal."

"I think I can do that. I'll grab a plunger on my way home from work, and I'll see you later. Come on, Munchkin. We better get moving, or I'll be late for work. Catch you later, Cam." She strolled away casually but couldn't resist looking over her shoulder to catch one last glimpse of him.

He was watching her walk away.

Damn!

A frisson of excitement skittered down her spine. She snapped her head around to the front and increased her pace. She shouldn't have let him catch her ogling him. Gosh darn it anyway. The man was too cute and too kind for his own good. And definitely too cute for her sanity. What was she going to do with him?

Lascivious thoughts rolled through her head, and she slipped on a patch of ice on the sidewalk. Dang it all! If she didn't watch herself, he'd make her do something stupid, like trip. Or kiss him. Not happening. Not now. Not tonight. Not ever. He was a great guy, but she wanted more than he seemed prepared to give.

The annoying voice in her head suggested he'd always been there to help her out and was going out of his way to make living next to a construction zone easier on her. She shushed the voice ruthlessly.

After work, Cam stopped by and made short work of unclogging the toilet. Patiently, he worked with Amy then gave her an explanation on how a toilet worked and why you didn't flush things that weren't meant to go in a toilet. He left with a promise to stop by for payment later.

By ten in the evening, Lisa was pacing restlessly. She was beyond ready for bed, and he hadn't shown up yet. The café had been a zoo all day, and work had passed in a rush. Another rig move. Rig moves were great. The entire crew stopped at once to rest and eat. Time flew when she was busy, and rig workers always tipped well. Being run off her feet didn't keep her from wondering why Cam's crew hadn't come in for lunch. She'd have to get a grip on her wayward thoughts. She'd messed up three orders today. It was a darn good thing Clint didn't expect her to pay for her screw-ups.

A soft knock sounded on the front door.

Finally.

She opened it and let Cam inside.

"Good Lord, you're filthy." He was mud from head to toe. Globs of concrete decorated his jacket and boots. There was even some kind of white goo in his hair.

"Don't I know it? I won't stay. I just stopped to say I wouldn't make it."

"Don't be silly. Hang on. I'll grab something for you to wear long enough to eat." She raced down the hall and returned with a fuzzy pink bathrobe.

"You want me to wear that?" He eyed it warily. "Do you have any idea how emasculating that thing is?"

"It's not like I have a men's wear department in my closet. And it's only a bit pink and fuzzy."

"A bit pink? It's screaming, cut-off-your-manhood pink."

"Well, it's big enough...sort of. You need to eat, and if you leave now, you won't get anything before breakfast." She hung the robe on a hook. "I'll go in the kitchen and warm up the soup. You get into the robe and wash your hands."

Soft shifting sounds and the thump of boots hitting the floor sounded behind her. It took everything she had not to turn around and steal a peek at him undressing.

"Good Lord." His grunt of disgust came from the kitchen doorway.

She turned and looked at him. The robe barely met over his chest, and if he moved wrong, she'd get a glimpse of his underwear and all they contained. His bare legs were fuzzy and muscular. His arms and shoulders threatened to explode from the tight confines of the robe.

"You look good in pink." She chuckled at his glare. "Oh my," she choked out between laughs. "I knew you were big, but geez…"

"Stuff it. I should have gone home instead."

"Okay, I'll try to contain myself." She bit back another laugh and put his soup on the table alongside a Caesar salad. "Eat up. Pasta'll be ready in a minute. Do you want a drink?"

"Yes. Please."

"Coffee, tea, juice or soda? I have a bottle of wine, and maybe, something harder." She opened the cupboard above the fridge.

"Soda is good. Something without caffeine, please. I'm bushed, but I don't need caffeine to keep me awake tonight."

Keeping half an eye on his exposed chest, she watched him settle at the table. Hot damn. She'd like to lick that. She fumbled with the ice cubes for his drink.

"You okay?" he asked with a raised eyebrow.

"Good. Fine." She set the glass on the table and served him a generous portion of chicken fettuccine with Alfredo sauce.

"Don't forget. I have a sister. I know what fine means to a woman—anything but fine—but keep your secrets because that smells great and I'm starving. And this soup is delicious. Tomato basil, unless I miss my guess, and homemade, too."

"It is. Although, I'll admit it was frozen. Left over from a couple weeks ago. I usually make a big batch of something and freeze it for later. I love cooking, but I'm more of a baker. I cook big and freeze it. Except cookies. There's nothing better than cookies hot out of the oven…" She trailed off. "Sorry. I'm babbling."

He laughed, his eyes lighting up and crinkling at the corners. "Nervous?"

"No. Maybe. Yes." She sighed.

"It's okay. You put me off my game, too." He shoveled in some more soup and took a bite of salad. "I'm attracted to you, but you scare the hell out of me."

What did he mean? She was hardly intimidating.

"How could I possibly scare you?"

"Crazy, right?" He ate a few bites more. "You're a little bit of a thing, but you scare me spitless sometimes." He looked down at the table.

"Little bit of a thing? I'm five seven."

"And I'm over six feet. Trust me; you're small."

"And you're scared of little ol' me?" She effected a poor excuse for a deep-South accent.

"Yes and no. Physically, no. I could take you anytime I wanted to."

She swallowed hard at the double entendre of his words.

"I didn't mean it like that. But you make me want things I don't want." He shrugged and took a long drink from his glass.

"Does make sense?" she asked, despite knowing exactly what he meant. Not that she'd admit it. She wanted him all hot and steamy in her bed, but she wanted and deserved more. She wouldn't let him detract her from her long-term goals. Even if she'd give almost anything for one shot at his body.

Hell's bells! It was a good thing she wasn't Catholic, or she'd have to go to confession for all these lustful thoughts. With effort, she turned her thoughts from using him.

"Sorry. That was inappropriate and unworthy of you," he

mumbled. "I don't mean to be an ass, but like I said, you put me off my game."

"How about we drop it?" It was as much an order as a question. "How was work?"

"Freaking awful." He laughed wryly. "The concrete truck backed too close to the pit and collapsed part of one wall. Thankfully, not badly. Then it leaked liquid cement down the side of the pit. Shoveling that up was no picnic. It was just one of those days." He fell silent.

"The kind of day that drives you to distraction and makes you want to pull your hair out?" She chuckled. "Boy, do I know that kind of day. And you look like you tried to pull your hair out. Is there concrete in your hair? Don't you wear a hard hat?"

"Usually, but it fell off twice today, for the first time ever. I felt like a green recruit with no idea what the hell I was doing."

"Makes for a long day. You must be exhausted," she commiserated.

"You know, I was, but now, I feel better. Still tired, but not dead on my feet. I'm sure I could rustle up the energy to steal a kiss."

"I think not." She tried for a haughty no-nonsense tone and knew she failed when he laughed.

"Lisa, sweetheart, I'm not taking anything you aren't willing to give." Then abruptly, he changed the subject. "Did Amy have any trouble going to sleep?"

"Surprisingly, no. She fell asleep right away. I was braced for a long fight that didn't happen. I got myself worked up for nothing."

They laughed together.

Much later, they stood at the front door. She'd kept busy in the kitchen while he'd changed back into his work clothing.

"So, thanks for dinner and the company. I enjoyed them both immensely. You're a good cook."

She blushed. "Thank you. I'm glad you came. Thanks for fixing the toilet earlier."

He leaned toward her, just a fraction of an inch, and she found herself leaning in to meet him for a kiss she wasn't sure she wanted. He disappointed her.

He inched back from her. One long, strong finger traced a line down her cheek and under her chin. She almost growled in frustration until he leaned in again then brushed his lips lightly across hers. It wasn't a kiss. It was more a feather-light touch which just about knocked her socks off.

Wow.

"Goodnight, beautiful. Sleep well. Dream about me." He laughed lightly then disappeared out the door, pulling it softly closed behind him.

CHAPTER 22

*L*isa shut off the blow dryer and called out to Amy. "Come brush your teeth. Time to get ready for daycare." When no answer came, she called again. Surely, Amy hadn't fallen back asleep after breakfast. "I better go wake her up."

She tossed her brush on the counter and headed for the living room.

The TV was on, the tinkle of animated chatter filled the room, but Amy wasn't on the couch or in the recliner. Or in the kitchen.

Lisa's parenting instincts kicked into overdrive. Unease skittered down her spine. Where had Amy gone?

She raced to the bedroom, calling out as she went. No sign of her anywhere.

"Shit. Amy, get out here." Fear and anger made her voice hard, even to her own ears. It wasn't like Amy to disappear. She always told Lisa where she was playing.

The basement!

Rushing downstairs, she shouted for Amy and searched frantically without success. What the hell did she do now? As she came back upstairs, a chill washed over her. Fear? Panic? Dread? Yes to all, but there was something else.

A draft drifted in from the patio door off the kitchen. She raced to the window. It was open just a sliver. She'd closed and locked it last night. She knew she had. She checked all the windows every night. Why was it ajar?

Outside, on the deck, in last night's fresh snow, were small footprints. They looked like bare feet, not boots. And they were too small to be made by an adult. Fresh snow was falling in heavy flakes and already obscuring the tracks.

"Oh my God. No!"

Snatching a coat off the rack beside the door, she slammed the door open and raced outside screaming for Amy.

She froze on the pinnacle of the steps and frantically scanned the yard. "Amy? Amy, where are you? Get back here, right now."

Her eyes caught a shadow, a hint of a depression in the snow near the corner of the house. She exploded off the step and sprinted across the yard to the spot.

There! Another footprint. Headed toward the gate that was open just an inch or so. Why was the gate open? She always closed the gate, and Amy couldn't reach the latch.

Dear God! What if someone had snuck in and abducted Amy.

Lisa bolted through the gate, her gaze slashing back and forth, searching for footprints, for any sign Amy had passed this way. She rushed through the space between her house and the neighbors', moving as fast as she could without risking missing something important.

She exploded around the corner into the front yard and jerked to a halt, her eyes scanning in every direction, searching for motion, for anything that might lead her to Amy.

"Amy!" She shouted her daughter's name repeatedly, her voice rising and becoming increasingly hoarse with each repetition.

"Lisa?"

She jerked her head toward the voice.

Cam.

"Lisa, what's wrong with Amy?" He raced up to her and grabbed her by the shoulders. "What?"

"She's gone!" Lisa pushed the words out past the constriction in her throat. She tried to jerk free of his grasp. He held tight. "Let go of me! I have to find her. Dammit, get out of my way."

"Lisa," he barked right into her face. "Stop. I'll help you. Tell me what's going on."

Tears rolled down her cheeks. She dashed them away, clearing her blurred vision. "Amy. The patio was open and the gate…" She gasped for breath. "She's in bare feet."

"Did you check the house?"

"Of course, I did." Her voice squeaked in panic. "Let go of me."

"How do you know she came outside? She might have just opened the door and stayed inside."

She pushed his hands off her shoulders and bolted.

He grabbed her from behind, stopping her in her tracks.

"Lisa, listen to me! If she's outside, we have to be calm. We'll find her. Show me what you saw."

A small part of her mind knew he was right. She had to be calm. But dammit, her daughter was missing. "I saw her footprints on the deck and coming this way. I was drying my hair—oh my God. It's my fault! I should have been watching her."

"Show me the tracks."

"There." She pointed to a slight depression in the snow. "They're already filling in. I have to go." Oh God, what if Amy got hurt or frostbit or worse?

"I'm going to call for help." He yanked out his cell phone and dialed. "Get everyone out here. Lisa's daughter is missing. We need to find her. Get everyone over here then call the police and tell them a four-year-old is missing."

Seconds later, a team of men streamed out of the construction site next door and assembled in front of them. Cam flipped through the photos on his phone and held the phone up. "This is Amy. She's four. She slipped out of this house, and we can't find her. Spread out. Look for her. We have to hurry. It's freezing out here, and we're pretty sure she doesn't have shoes on. And maybe, not a coat. Some of you follow those small tracks. Go."

Lisa watched them scatter and wrapped her arms around herself. It was so cold outside, and inside, her heart chilled even more. "I have to look."

Cam stopped her with a hand on her shoulder. "You have to stay here; talk to the police. Get a picture from inside. Come on. I'll help you search the house again."

Gently, he spun her to face him. His gaze caught hers. His eyes reflected her fears. He was afraid for her daughter. Compassion and sympathy were there, too. His concern helped her reach for rationality. She didn't find true calm, but levelheadedness crept in. Losing control wouldn't help.

"Come on inside. We'll look again. We'll find her. The police will be here soon."

His hand was warm and comforting in hers as he led her around to the back of the house and inside. He slipped out of his coat and boots and helped her shed her drenched slippers.

"Okay, one room at a time. We start here. Every cupboard, every closet, every shelf. Look beneath everything. Even the refrigerator."

"The fridge?" Her voice squeaked in surprise.

"Yeah. My nephew once climbed into the fridge, playing hide and seek. He fell asleep there. If it weren't for the milk he spilled getting in, I don't know how long he'd have stayed there before Ang found him. His brother had stopped looking, distracted by cartoons."

The image made her stomach clench. Dear God. Kids could be such trouble.

She didn't relax much, but it helped that he was there trying so hard to keep her calm and helping her look.

They searched the entire house. Under the beds, in closets, in tight corners too small to hide a child. As they finished, sirens sounded, and someone hammered on the front door.

"That'll be the police." He grabbed her hand and led her to the door.

"Hi, Mac." Lisa tried to smile at RCMP Officer, McKenzie Stewart, and his partner, Betty Lawson. "Come in." She backed away so they could enter. "Coffee?" she asked, fighting for something, anything, to calm herself.

"In a bit." Betty smiled comfortingly. "We need to organize a search. But first a few questions."

"Come on, Lisa. Sit down." Cameron led her to the sofa, his hand warm and comforting in hers. He handed Mac a recent picture of Amy.

"Okay, Lisa. Tell it to us from the beginning."

"She's been gone for a while." She looked at her watch. "Twenty minutes. I was drying my hair; she was watching TV. Oh God, I should have been watching her." She wailed and choked back tears.

"That's your usual routine?" Mac asked softly.

"It is. I didn't think she could open the patio. I'm sure it was locked. And for some reason, the gate was open. I know she can't reach that." She leapt to her feet and paced the room.

"Come on, Sweetie. Relax." Cam patted the couch beside him. "Let's talk this out, so the full search can start. We've sent my employees searching. They'll call in if they find her," Cam added.

Lisa perched uncomfortably on the edge of the seat, her legs twitching and bouncing, her arms wrapped around her middle. Slowly, she recounted the past half hour, blaming herself every step of the way.

"This isn't your fault." Cam tried to reassure her. "One thing, probably the only thing I know about kids, is that they always find a way to distress their parents. We'll get through this. We'll find our girl."

Her cell phone rang from the kitchen. She leaped up, grabbed it and glanced at the display.

Clint. Her boss. Shit. She'd forgotten to call him.

"Clint. Hi." In as few words as possible, she explained the situation and begged forgiveness. She listened for a moment. "Thanks."

Five minutes later, he was at the door with a dozen people standing behind him.

"What's the plan, Mac? Where should we start looking?" Clint asked.

"Come inside. We'll set up a command center in the dining room."

In minutes, they had the town divided into grids and people dispatched to their designated areas.

Lisa pulled on her coat.

"Where do you think you're going?" Cam asked.

"To find my daughter," she snapped. "I need to look."

"You need to be here when we find her," Mac corrected. "And we need to know her favorite places to visit and her friends."

"Come back inside, Lisa. They'll find her. We'll get her back. Take your coat off. Come into the dining room. Or start phoning your friends to see if they've seen her."

Reluctantly, she followed them inside.

"Take your coat off." Cam tried to help her out of it.

"I can't. I'm freezing." She shivered under the heavy jacket.

"I'll turn up the heat and get you coffee." He disappeared and returned with coffee and a bulky sweater. "Put this on instead. It'll keep you warm. The heat's up."

Vainly, she called everyone she knew. They agreed to keep their eyes open and help with the search.

How could one girl disappear so quickly, so thoroughly?

Two hours later, people trickled in to report the bad news. There was no sign of her. Nick, from the bakery, arrived with trays of sandwiches and cookies for the volunteers. Clint showed up with thermoses, coffee and a high-speed, industrial coffeemaker. He showed Harmony how it worked and left to help search. The house swarmed with people coming and going.

Lisa paced, rocking back and forth on her feet, clutching at any glimmer of hope or stray thought that might calm her. She needed to be out looking. Amy needed her, but they wouldn't let her go.

"Drink this." Cam handed her a mug of tea. "It'll calm you."

She cradled the cup but didn't sip the beverage. Its warmth seeped into her hands, taking off the icy feel but doing nothing to warm the chill in her heart. If anything happened to Amy, she'd never forgive herself.

Cam led her to the couch and sat down, drawing her down beside him, tight against his side. "Come on, honey. You need to relax. Cuddle in here, and I'll warm you up." He wrapped a blanket around her shoulders and pulled her up tight.

Tears trickled down her face, and shivers racked her body. Anger, fear, helplessness and hopelessness chased each other through her mind. Her chest was tight, breathing becoming increasingly difficult. She tried to swallow the lump in her throat. It didn't budge. It lodged there, threatening to choke her.

Cam whispered nonsensical words in her ear and stroked her back and hair. It was comforting, as if she didn't have to go through this alone. Her chills eased in the warmth of his embrace, and her tears slowed. Panic still raced inside her, but with effort, she was able to bank it down, push it to the back burner and gather a sense of calm. Not true calm, but the façade of calm. She felt almost…functional.

Someone handed her a sandwich. Roast beef and cheese. She knew it was delicious because Nick's Bakery never made anything that wasn't, but for all she knew, it might have been made of cardboard. She choked it down anyway.

"I need coffee," she muttered.

"How many cups do you drink in a day?"

She gave Cam a puzzled look. "Three at the most."

"Do you really think you need more? You've had three since I got here. And tea. You're wired and twitchy. Coffee won't help."

Harmony came up to them and handed her a glass of orange

juice. "Drink this. It'll keep the thirst down. Save the caffeine for later. I'd give you a shot of brandy, but the good doc there won't let me." She waved vaguely to the corner of the room.

Lisa followed the gesture. The doc was here? When had he arrived? No doubt, someone had thought she was losing it and called him. She scanned the room. Wow. There were over a dozen people here, busy with various tasks, and there was no telling how many were searching. And here she sat, doing nothing. She had to help search.

Slipping out of Cam's arms, she mustered up a smile. It was wobbly at best. "I have to look for her. I can't stay here."

"And when they find her? When she needs you, where will you be? Out there somewhere?" He gestured widely encompassing the whole town.

"I'll take my phone. I'll leave the number."

"You need to stay." His calm voice grated on her nerves.

"You need to shut the hell up. I need to go. I'm going. I don't care what you or anyone else thinks. This is my daughter," she sobbed. "I can't stay and do nothing. This is my fault, and I have to fix it. I have to find her."

She whirled around, scanning the room. "Grace? You have my cell number. Call me if they find her first." With that, she snatched up a coat, slipped into some boots and bolted out the front door with no particular direction in mind.

"Wait. Lisa. Wait. I'll come with you. We'll look together," Cam called after her. She paused only a fraction of a second. Just long enough to hear him mutter, "The last thing we need is you lost, too."

"Seriously?" She whirled and glared. "Don't start."

He held up his placating hands. "I'm worried about you both. Sue me. Now, where do you want to start? Is there someplace she likes to go that you didn't mention before?"

"No. I don't think so." She paused then smiled. "Yes!" She

jogged off as fast as she could in her heavy boots. "Wilkersons' barn."

"Is it far? Could she make it alone?"

"I don't think so, but we've been there dozens of times. And last night, she was talking about kittens. They had kittens last time we were there. Let's go."

"Wait. We'll take my truck. It'll be faster, even if we go slowly. Call ahead. Let them know to start looking."

They raced down the street and jumped into his truck. He blasted away from the curb before she even had her seatbelt on. There was no answer when she called the farm. As Cam drove, Lisa called out directions. It was a bit farther by road than by the bike path they usually walked, and it seemed like an eternity before they arrived.

"Over there, by the barn behind the house." She waved wildly, and he skidded to a stop.

They leapt out of the truck and raced to the barn, flinging open the door and shouting for Amy. It was pitch dark inside but slightly warmer than outside.

"Lights. I'll get the lights." She fumbled around, glad she'd been here several times before. Finally, she located the switch by the small door.

Light exploded into the room, and a dog growled near the back of the barn by the tack room.

"That's Gravy."

"Gravy?"

"Wilkersons' dog."

Cam laughed despite the dire situation. "There's got to be a story behind that. Is he mean?"

She raced toward the growling. "She's a sweetie. Gravy, stop growling. You know me." She slid into the tack room. Gravy growled louder, and Lisa slowed to a stop. "It's okay, girl. It's me. Lisa. I'm looking for Amy."

She didn't take her eyes from the dog. She felt Cam come up

behind her, and Gravy growled louder and bared her teeth. Moving slowly, Lisa held out her hand, fingers curled under and inched toward the dog. "Come on, girl. Is she here? Is my baby here?"

"There. In the corner," Cam whispered. "Under the blanket. Is that a mitten?"

She took another small step forward, and Gravy hunkered down, placing herself between Lisa and the blanket.

Outside, vehicle doors slammed, and a voice called out, "Hey, you. In the barn. Get out here."

"That's Stan Wilkerson." She kept her eyes on the dog. "Stan, it's me. Lisa Brown. Amy's missing, and Gravy won't let me search for her."

Limping footsteps hurried toward them. "Gravy, stand down."

The dog stopped growling but didn't move until her master came in sight.

"Come." Stan patted his leg.

Gravy cast a wary glance at Lisa but obeyed. The dog walked over to Stan and sat at his feet.

"What's up, girl?" Stan patted Gravy's head.

Lisa moved toward the blanket, calling out softly. "Amy? Mommy's here. Come out, sweetie."

Gravy growled again, and Stan shushed her.

"Mommy?"

The blankets stirred, and Amy's sleepy, straw-covered hair poked out from under the blankets.

"Oh, baby. Come here." She held out her hands, and Amy rushed into them.

"Mommy, it was so cold, but Gravy kept me warm."

"Amy, you are in such big trouble for leaving the house." She hugged her close. "But I'm so glad you're safe. Why did you leave the house?"

"I saw the cat. I followed her. Muffin is my friend. I followed her. But then I gotted lost. I saw the barn and 'membered it. I came here. I crawled in the doggy door, and Gravy came, too."

Relief and anger washed over Lisa. Her baby was safe but had committed a grievous error in leaving the house.

"Mommy, why you crying?"

Lisa wiped her tears on her sleeve. "I'm crying because I'm so happy you're safe. And so angry you went outside alone. And so glad Gravy kept you warm."

"Gravy showed me the blanket. It was a long walk, and I gotted tired."

Lisa turned to Stan. "Sorry for the trouble."

"No worries. I'm glad the little one is safe. Bring her back for a visit sometime."

"We'll do that. Thanks so much," Lisa replied graciously.

"Come on, ladies. Let's get you home." Cam slipped off his coat and handed it to Lisa. "I called Sterling. He's calling off the search. And you, young lady, have an appointment with the doctor and the police."

Amy's face blanched. "The police?" she whispered.

"And the doctor. He has to check that you didn't get hurt or freeze your feet," Lisa added. It was perversely pleasing that Amy was scared of the police. She'd been taught to respect them and listen to them. Hopefully this would be just the scare she needed to prevent a repeat of today's disaster.

"My feet got cold. I putted my mittens on them." She smiled proudly, clearly pleased with her initiative. "I forgot my coat." She looked down as if embarrassed by her mistake.

Lisa looked down and laughed at the sight of her daughter's feet wearing mittens like socks. "That's pretty smart thinking." She wrapped Amy in Cam's coat and lifted her up.

She stumbled on the uneven barn floor.

"Here, let me take her before you fall." Cam scooped Amy out of Lisa's arms. He gave them both a warm smile. "It's been a long day. I'll give her back when we get to the truck."

The truck was still running and had warmed up considerably since they abandoned it a few moments before. Cam settled them both in with a kiss to the forehead. He rounded the truck and climbed in on the other side.

Lisa looked at him, smiling softly. He looked tired. God, she was exhausted. Amy was already asleep in her arms.

"Thanks, Cameron. I couldn't have survived the day without you." He'd been a knight in shining armor, there through the whole trying day. He'd been strong when she was weak. Useful when she was helpless. He'd been her rock.

Leaning over, she kissed him on the cheek and stroked his hair. "I'm so glad you were there. Thank you."

He looked her in the eye and studied her face as if he were looking for something. A warm smile turned up the corner of his mouth. "Glad to help." He leaned in and kissed her on the lips.

Shivers raced through her for the hundredth time since she'd noticed Amy was gone, but this was different. This was warm and caring. Tenderness washed over her, and she leaned into him. "Take us home, Sir Galahad."

He laughed at that, his low chuckle heating her body and warming her heart.

Putting the truck in gear, he winked and said, "I wish I could, Princess. But Amy needs to see the doctor, and the police will probably want to clear things up."

"To the clinic then. You know where it is?" She didn't need this. All she wanted was a good stiff drink and a thirty-six-hour nap.

CHAPTER 23

Doc Hardy met them at the clinic door.

"Doc, this is Sterling's friend, Cameron Zeus. You might remember him from Grace and Sterling's wedding. He helped me find Amy." She nodded from one to the other.

They shook hands.

"I've run into Cam a few times."

"I met Doc ages ago when a worker got hurt on the job and then met him again at the wedding."

"I remember that you were going to fire the guy that got hurt." That still annoyed her.

"Not really. I was just pissed. I'd never can someone because of a single accident. Though I have given the boot to guys who repeatedly caused accidents. Everyone makes mistakes." He shrugged.

"Come on, bring little missy into the back, and I'll give her the once-over."

"Do you mind if I tag along?" Cam looked at both Doc and Lisa for approval.

He'd been there for her all day. She could hardly kick him out now. She nodded, and he followed them down the short hallway.

169

"So, Amy," Doc said after he'd closed the door behind them. "What mischief have you gotten yourself into?"

"I followed a kitty and got lost." She hung her head.

"What are you going to do next time you see a cat?" he asked as he examined her feet.

"Tell Mommy before I go outside," she whispered.

The shame and fear in her voice cut straight into Lisa's heart. God, it hurt so badly when her baby was hurting. She knew she should be thankful Amy was unharmed, but anger lurked in the back of her heart. She had no idea how to deal with this mix of emotions.

"You do that. You know the rules," Doc said. "Never go anywhere without telling Mommy first. Does this hurt?" He poked at her toes with his pen.

"It tickles." She pulled her foot back and giggled.

He poked some more, checked out her hands and arms and listened to her chest. "Fit as a fiddle," he declared at last. "But you should watch out for chills or a fever, just to be on the safe side. Give her a warm bath, some food and get her into bed."

Relief flooded through Lisa, and her knees went weak. She stumbled, and Cam grasped her by the arm, holding her upright. His hand was warm and gentle and gave her a feeling of security she resented.

"Are you okay?" He looked her in the eye.

"I'm fine."

"Liar," he said softly. "You're anything but fine."

"It's just stress." She shook off his arm. "I'll be okay after I rest a bit."

He studied her up and down before nodding solemnly. "I won't leave you alone until you're ready for bed then."

"I'll be fine. You can go back to work."

"Girl, the workday is done. And I'm not leaving you alone. You've had an ass-kicking of a day. I'll feed you and tuck you both in. Then I'll leave you alone. Maybe."

"Cam…" God, she didn't need him hovering over her.

"He's right. You both need a little adult supervision and some support while dealing with the RCMP. Consider it doctor's orders to keep him around for the evening."

"I don't need help."

"Probably not, but I'm insisting." The doctor put away his stethoscope and looked at Cam. "You take care of these two lovely ladies."

"Will do."

Lisa sighed heavily. Good grief, men were such an irritant. She didn't need to hang around Cam any more than was absolutely necessary. He'd been a godsend today, but the very last thing she wanted was to become dependent on a love-'em-and-leave-'em guy like him. Time to change the subject and hope they both forgot about babysitting her.

"So, I hear there's a doula in town."

Doc made a disgruntled sound.

"What's a doula?" Cam asked.

"A pain in the ass who gets in a proper doctor's way." Doc humphed.

"A doula is like a midwife. She helps with pregnancy, delivery and after care," Lisa said, glaring at the doctor. "What have you got against that?"

"Pregnant women need proper care, not some medical school dropout meddling in their affairs."

"Wow. Harsh." Cam chuckled.

"Have you even met her? Or are you just judging her blindly?" Lisa gave him her best parenting eyeball.

"Don't need to meet her to know she's a hack." He crossed his arms over his chest.

"Oh my God. Save me from idiot men." She shook her head. "Come on, Amy. Time to go home." Lifting her daughter from the exam table, Lisa left Cameron and the doctor behind.

In the lobby, she waited for Cameron to catch up. She'd have left without him, but she didn't have a vehicle. She was trapped and wanted nothing more than to be free of domineering men and to have a glass of wine. Or a shot of whiskey.

Her cell phone rang as she climbed into the truck. When she peeked at the call display, her home number had appeared. Good grief. She thumbed the screen and took the call. It was Mac on the other end, telling her he'd wait at her house until she got home. They could straighten things out then.

Mac didn't have any questions for Amy, but he gave her a stern warning. She teared up and promised to tell her mother where she was going. After calming Amy down, Lisa gave her a snack then tucked her in bed before sitting down to talk to Mac. All in all, it didn't take long to deal with his paperwork and to reassure him everything was fine. Despite the brevity of the task, it was a relief to finally shut the door behind him.

CHAPTER 24

Cam slipped into the kitchen while Lisa saw Mac to the door. McKenzie Stewart was a good man. Friendly and helpful, even as he was all business. It was easy to see why Grace and Sterling thought so highly of him. He was just one of the reasons Sterling was moving the company to Haven. Sterling had offered to let Cam run the city office, but so far, Cam was undecided. They didn't need two offices.

Could he live in this backwoods town? There were lots of great people here, like Mac. He'd make a good friend. Cam pushed that thought away. Sure, Sterling was moving his company to Haven, but that didn't mean Cam was moving with it. He had a life in the city. He was a single man on the prowl, looking for a good time. There were bars to visit and women to date.

Yeah, but if he didn't move to Haven, he wouldn't see Lisa all the time. He'd gotten used to seeing her at the café and ruffling her feathers. She was sweet and kind. Her sense of humor was a bit twisted sometimes, but she made him laugh. He liked that she could laugh at herself as easily as she laughed at others. He'd definitely miss her when he left this town in his dust.

173

Or, the little voice in his head suggested, *you could just stay here. Move to Haven. Settle down and make a family of your own.*

Hell no!

He didn't want long term. He'd tried that with Kim. Epic failure. He'd just keep on dating and enjoy his family time with his sister and her kids. He didn't need a family of his own. Nope. No freaking way. No how. Not ever.

"You look deep in thought. What's on your mind?" Lisa's voice startled him back to the present.

"It's been a long day. Can I get you some wine?" He didn't look at her. He couldn't. She was perceptive and might see the turmoil in his mind.

"So, that's how it is? You just avoid my question?" She looked at him with that parent-eye she had down pat.

He said nothing, just held up the wine in questioning.

"Fine. I'd love a glass of wine. I need it. I need a barrel of wine."

He poured them both a large glass of Cabernet just as the doorbell rang. "I'll get that. It's probably the pizza I ordered. I hope that's okay. I'm starving."

"Me, too. Thanks. I don't think I'm up to a decision right now. I just want to shut down and stop thinking."

He went to the door, paid for the pizza then returned to the living room. She hadn't moved an inch. He paused and studied her. Her eyes were almost closed, her head tipped to one side to rest against the back of the sofa, her arms were limp, and she looked seconds away from sleep. Indecision caught him square in the gut. Should he wake her? Should he feed her?

She'd said she was starving. She'd hardly eaten all day. The stress had knocked her on her ass. She'd been dumping adrenaline all day, so the fall must be brutal. Yup, she needed food then a good twelve hours of shuteye. He placed the pizza on the coffee table and went into the kitchen for plates and napkins. While there, he called Sterling and suggested a late start to the workday tomorrow. If the crew kept the noise down she'd be able to catch a little extra sleep.

His sister still had nightmares about the time her son had gone missing, and he'd only been gone for about half an hour. To have a child lost for several hours could leave long-term scars. There had to be a way to ease the burden of what they'd been through. Amy, no doubt, would pull through like a trooper. It was Lisa who had him worried.

She was awake when he returned to the living room.

"Morning, Sleeping Beauty," he teased her.

"Sorry. I guess I'm more tired than I'd thought."

"It's been a long day for you. No shame in needing some sleep." He settled on the floor between the sofa and the coffee table. She slid down to join him.

"I need food more. Is this thing loaded?" She popped open the pizza box. "Meat, veggies and cheese. Oh God, yes. Does it get any better than this?"

He swallowed hard. Damn, she sounded like a woman having an orgasm. And now, he couldn't get that image out of his head. Shit.

"Give me a piece of that before you inhale the whole thing," he teased.

She held the box out of his reach. "What's it worth to you?"

"Don't make me force you to give it back." He made a mock lunge for the box.

"Nope. Nope." She waggled her finger under his nose. "This delicious, cheesy goodness is mine. All mine."

"Then you leave me with no option but to take it from you."

She laughed at him.

He dove toward her, but instead of grabbing the pizza, he clutched her shoulders and pressed his lips against hers. Her breath squeaked out in surprise, and she softened against him. In an instant, she went from roughhousing to soft compliance, and from there, to eager participation.

The pizza box hit the table with a thud, and her arms slid around his shoulders, drawing him closer. Arousal ratcheted up his spine, shuddering through him, lodging in his groin. Oh crap. He didn't need this temptation. And she was tempting. Entirely too tempting. He should back away. He really should.

But, damn, her lips felt too good against him. Too soft, too delicious, too perfect. He pushed the table away. Leaning in, he grasped her by the waist and pulled her onto his lap. He had to stop this. She was reacting to the day's stress. She didn't want him. She wanted distraction.

Since when did he care? Wasn't he all about stealing a moment in time and enjoying the passion? Maybe in the past, but right now, right here, with Lisa…not so much.

Slowly, gently, he planted little kisses on her cheeks, up her hairline then paused with his lips pressed against her forehead. "We can't do this."

She spun on his lap to straddle him. She ground against his arousal. Her heat burned him even through their jeans. Damn.

"Why not?" she asked, moving her hips in slow circles. "We're both consenting adults. I need you. I can feel that you want me."

"It's the stress." He swallowed hard. "You just want a distraction."

"Is that so bad?" She cupped his face between her palms and brought her lips to his. She brushed their lips together softly, gently then devoured his.

He resisted. For a second. And then he gave into the temptation. He kissed her hard and deep, their tongues dancing. Tasting, giving, taking. Her hands dropped from his face to fumble with his belt.

Jesus!

"Hey. Hey. Come on, Lisa. Slow down. This isn't what you want. It isn't right. You deserve better than a quickie on the floor. You deserve someone who will love you forever." A little voice in his head whispered that he could love her.

She leaned back and fixed him with a glare. "Don't you want me?" she demanded.

"Fuck yes."

"Then what's the problem?" She smirked at him. "Are ya chicken?"

"No. But…"

"Do you have a condom?" she persisted.

"I do, but that's not the point." God, how did he distract her? He had to get out of here before he did something stupid…like make love to her.

"What's the issue? I thought you liked me. You, Mr. Love-'em-and-leave-'em. We're both consenting adults. You've got protection. I want you." She ground against him, sending his blood pounding through his veins. "You want me."

Then she did the one thing he couldn't resist. She looked up at him with soft, pleading eyes and whispered, "Please."

Her arms snaked around him, and she lowered herself onto her back on the floor, leading him down atop her. He closed his eyes, hoping to find the strength to refuse her. It was no good. His moral compass had flown out the window with her inhibitions. Damn.

He pulled away and eased himself to his feet. Offering his hand, he whispered, "For you, just this once. But not here. Not on the floor. You deserve to be made love to properly, on a bed."

Grasping his hand, she scrambled to her feet and led him into the bedroom.

CHAPTER 25

She should feel bad about this, about seducing him, but she didn't. Searching deep, she looked for warning signs, for unease. She found none. She wanted him; he wanted her. They were adults. There was nothing to feel guilty about. There was no reason to resist the passion arcing between them. He followed her into the bedroom without comment and eased the door shut behind them.

She led him to the bed then rummaged through a drawer. With a flick of her thumb, her lighter flared to life, and she lit the two candles on her nightstand then pulled the drapes shut. There wasn't a single doubt in her mind that this was right. She loved him. He might not love her, but there was no shame in sharing passion with the man you loved. Eager anticipation battled with her nerves. He was here, in her bedroom. Surely, he wouldn't reject her now. Would he?

Moving back to him, she raised up on her tiptoes and placed a soft kiss on his lips. "Make love to me, Cameron. Please."

Even in the dim light of the room, she saw the passion flare in his eyes. Her body responded with a surge of heat at her core.

Forcing herself to go slowly, she unbuttoned his shirt, kissing each tiny sliver of skin as it was exposed. Gosh, he was so delicious, so tasty. A hint of salt, a hint of man. She leaned in and licked his nipple. She chuckled at his sharp inhalation. Oh yeah, she had him. There was no way he'd turn her down now. She slipped his shirt off his shoulders and down his arms before dropping it carelessly on the floor.

She nibbled her way down his chest to the dark arrow of hair trailing into his jeans. She adored the contrast between the soft, smooth skin and the rough hair. Her lips and palms tingled.

"Come up here," he whispered, his voice low and hoarse. He grasped her arms, encouraging her to rise.

"I think not." She chuckled. "I'm quite happy where I am." She looked up at him and smiled. Holding his gaze with hers, she fumbled with his belt and finally managed to unfasten it. She slipped it open and delved back into working the buttons on his fly. Wow. A button fly. She didn't have much experience with those. But as he hardened under her fingertips and she worked the buttons, she decided she liked all those buttons. Sure a zipper was fast and easy, but this was a special torture for them both.

Buttons freed at last, she slipped her hands under his waistband and inched his jeans lower. She kissed his belly, tickling his navel with her tongue, and pressed her cheek against the burning heat of his arousal. He was rock hard. She felt his grunt more than she heard it. She pushed off his jeans and helped him step out of them.

"Come up here," he repeated. "I need to touch you."

She rose, trailing her lips up his body as she moved.

He flipped back the bedcovers then turned to her with a smile. He grasped the hem of her sweater and slipped it up and over her head. It landed on the floor near his discarded clothing.

She stood before him, in jeans and bra and let him look his fill. She'd expected to feel shy or reluctant, but all she felt was anticipation. His gaze felt like a brand on her skin. Her heartbeat accelerated, and a soft moan escaped her mouth.

"Jesus, you're beautiful." His hands cupped her breasts.

She liked how his dark tan contrasted with the pure white of her bra.

"And lace… Are you trying to kill me? You could give a man a heart attack."

"I thought you construction workers were stronger than that? I thought you were tough." She stifled a giggle at the thought of giving him a heart attack. He did have a way of making her laugh, and she liked knowing she aroused him. "Are you tough enough to follow through on this…or is your chicken heart going to pack up and run away?"

"Are you calling me weak? Or a chicken?" He growled low in his throat.

"If the beak fits— Ah!" Her breath whooshed out in a grunt when he tackled her and tossed her onto the bed.

He climbed up and straddled her, his legs on either side of her waist, his feet pinning down her legs. He grasped her hands and pinioned them over her head. Pausing, almost infinitesimally, he watched her, waiting for approval.

She arched up to kiss him. She pressed her lips against him and slipped her tongue inside his mouth. Tasting the wine and faint hint of mint she found there, she explored his soft lips, his firm tongue and the hardness of his teeth. She nibbled on his lips and whispered a chicken sound.

His eyes widened in surprise, and he laughed. "Is this how it's always going to be with you? Expect the unexpected? Giggles and laughs mixed with passion?" He punctuated each word with a kiss, slowly moving from her mouth, down her neck and trailing his lips along her collarbone.

Her mind fumbled for an amusing retort, but rational thought fled under the caress of his lips. She groaned. "Oh my, that feels so good."

Releasing her hands, he slid to the left, lying on his side and pressing up against her. His right leg draped over hers. Gazing into her eyes, he trailed one finger down the curve of her bra.

Her breath skittered from her lungs.

"What's this?" He looked down and fingered the plastic clasp between her breasts.

"Front opening," she panted.

He fumbled a minute more. "Damn."

"Like this." With a quick twist and a flip of her fingers, her bra popped open.

"Damn. I like that." He licked along the edge of the bra where it still clung to the small curves of her breasts. "So lovely. So soft. So warm."

His gaze found hers again. He must have read the uncertainty in her eyes. He whispered, "My God, Lisa, you're beautiful. So soft and feminine. But fit and strong, too."

His hands slid across her belly and followed the line of her jeans. "These have to go." He flicked the button open and slid down the zipper. "Lift," he commanded softly. She raised her hips, and he drew her jeans down inch by inch. He discarded them over the edge of the bed.

"God," he groaned. "More lace?"

His lips left a trail of moist fire where they traced across her belly. She giggled when he tickled her belly button with his tongue as he moved upward toward her breasts. The cups of her bra had slid aside, catching on her nipples. He tweaked them gently and suckled them through the lace.

She grasped his head, burying her fingers in his hair, drawing him up and kissing him firmly on the mouth. "You're…going… too…slow," she panted.

"What's the rush, Pixie-Sticks? We have all night."

"It's been a while. I need you." She blushed.

"It's been a long time for me, too. Longer than I want to admit. And I'm clean. I just had my physical."

"Mmm," she murmured against his lips. "But you have protection, so we're good."

"Better than good." His fingers traced designs over her arms and shoulders.

"It's been over three years for me, except for Bob."

He jerked back and stared at her. "Who the hell is Bob?"

She burst into giggles that quickly turned to a full belly laugh.

"Lisa, stop it. Who's Bob?"

"Bob is my boyfriend." She smirked at his pique.

"You have a boyfriend? I thought you were single. That's it. I'm out of here." He jerked to his feet and fumbled for his clothing.

"Wait." All her laughter disappeared at his haste to do the right thing. "I thought everyone knew about Bob." His glare squelched the last of her mirth. "Bob stands for battery-operated-boyfriend. Didn't you know that?"

"Jesus Murphy. How would I know that?" He dropped his pants and stalked back toward her. "You'll pay for teasing me like that." Kneeling beside the bed, he grasped her legs and yanked her to the edge. "Don't ever scare me like that again."

His words didn't come off as anger or selfishness. They rang of concern, relief and maybe a bit of possessiveness. She studied him. He wanted her, but not at the cost of another man's unhappiness. For a rogue, he sure was sweet.

She smiled. "Sorry."

In one swift, breathtaking move he had her panties off and his mouth on her mound. He went still against her, and his breath whispered across her heat. She barely heard his muffled groan before his lips touched her. The touch was moist, hot and electric, nearly jolting her off the bed.

His laughter tickled her thighs. "You'll pay for that."

He delved in, licking, sucking. Tasting. She writhed under his onslaught. Shards of electric pleasure wafted over her. Her nipples pinched tighter. Her skin prickled. Her breathing came in gasps. Wiggling and writhing, she tried to free herself before she went over the edge. He slipped her thighs over his shoulders and pulled her closer. With one hand on her belly, the other grasping her ankles behind his head, he feasted on her.

Whimpers of pleasure formed and dissipated as her arousal grew. It built and built. Just when she thought she could take no more, he eased off to nibble her thighs. The flood of unbearably hot sensations ebbed, and he dove in again. Pushing her to the edge then backing off. Closer and closer, he took her until she was lost, pitched over the edge into a swirling maelstrom of pleasure.

When she fluttered down to reality, she was snuggled up in his arms, his cock rigid against her thigh. She smiled up at him. He winked and gave her a smug smile in return. She swatted him on the arm.

"Good?" he teased.

"Glorious. But inadequate." She laughed at his mock indignation. "I think, perhaps, I need more."

"Now, *that* I can provide." He kissed her long and slow.

She read his emotions in that kiss. Tenderness. Caring. Passion. And something more? She blocked that thought and put her hands to use. Gracious, he was hot. Smooth skin, rough hair. His muscles bunched and flexed under her touch. She explored every inch of him with her fingers and mouth. Sliding out of his embrace, she knelt beside him on the bed, slipped off his briefs and tasted him. Salt and tang teased her tongue, fueling her arousal. Delicious.

She barely had him in her mouth when he eased away. "Not this time," he groaned. "I can't take it. Later. Maybe."

He grabbed his jeans from the floor and triumphantly extracted a condom.

"Let me." She snatched the packet from his hand and ripped it open with her teeth. She fumbled a bit getting it on him and apologized for her ineptitude.

"I don't want an expert. I want you."

Gently, he eased her onto her back and lay above her. They fit as if they were made for each other. Their curves and hollows meshed perfectly. She shifted under him, and his cock slid between her thighs. She twisted again, stroking him along her cleft. Another wiggle and he was nestled against her opening.

"Are you sure?"

She thrust her hips upward, wrapping her heat around him. "Shut up, Cam."

He obeyed. Not another word passed his lips. Moving slowly, cautiously, he eased himself into her a fraction of an inch at a time. He thrust in and out until he was finally seated fully then he smiled down at her and pressed a soft kiss to her forehead. "Okay?"

"Yes." Her cheeks heated. "More. Please."

They moved slowly, seeking. They fumbled for a moment until they found that one perfect rhythm that suited them both. Their strokes meshed as they came together. Fingers and lips wandered. Breaths escaped, becoming sighs and groans. Their slow movements quickened as their heat rose until at last she exploded over the edge with him just a breath behind her.

He stayed atop her until they recovered, keeping his weight on his elbows and knees. Slowly, he rolled to the side, taking her with him. She snuggled in close after passing him a tissue from the side table, and he made quick work of discarding the condom then pulled her tight against his chest. They lay together drifting slowly into sleep.

CHAPTER 26

Sometime later, Lisa woke up. She wasn't sure which was worse: the growling of her stomach or the pressure on her bladder. And she was hot. Too hot. Why was it so hot in her room? She moved to push down the covers and bumped into a hairy arm draped across her waist, pinning her in place.

Cam!

In her bed. Crap.

That explained the heat. She stopped wiggling. He was asleep, his arm wrapped around her. Her head was tucked up against his shoulder. Daylight crept in around the curtains.

What was he doing in her bed?

Memories flooded back. Hot, steamy, erotic and tender.

Holy hockey socks!

Had she actually seduced him?

Oh yeah.

Oh no!

She had.

And it was fabulous.

Moving inch by inch, she extracted herself from his embrace

and slipped off the bed. Her bladder was fit to burst, but it had nothing on the tangle of emotions battering her heart.

Oh gosh. This was a mistake. A huge mistake. What had she been thinking? She'd let her emotions get the better of her. In the aftermath of Amy's disappearance and return, she'd turned to Cameron for comfort and stability. He'd given her that and more. What the hell had she been thinking? She hadn't been drunk; she'd only had a few sips of wine.

She snuck out of the bedroom and into the main bathroom, grabbing her robe from the back of the door as she went. She used the bathroom and tidied herself up as best she could without making any noise. She wasn't ready to face him yet. She closed the lid on the unflushed toilet and sat down.

What the hell did she do now? Crap. Crap. Crap.

"Okay," she whispered to herself. "Think about this rationally. We're both adults. We went into this willingly. Nobody got hurt."

Her stomach cramped, and she sucked in a breath. She'd stepped in it this time. Now, all she had to do was extract herself from this without making matters worse. She had to get rid of him without revealing how deeply she'd fallen for him. And she sure wouldn't tell him she'd had the best orgasms of her life last night. She'd just keep that tidbit to herself.

She slipped from the bathroom, tiptoed to the kitchen and started some coffee. She'd give him coffee and breakfast, hopefully before Amy woke up, then she'd send him on his way. She just had to get rid of him without causing grief for either one of them.

Her heart clenched at the thought. She didn't want to be free of him. He'd been amazing yesterday. So strong and caring.

And last night? Hell's bells. He'd been a considerate and generous lover. She'd drifted off in his arms afterward, feeling cherished and appreciated. She wouldn't even think about how well he'd satisfied her.

Good grief. She had to stop thinking about his effect on her. Cam wasn't hers, and he never would be. But he'd been such a blessing yesterday. He'd kept his head when hers had threatened to explode from fear and panic. She would have lost her mind without him and everyone else who'd pitched in to help out. Most of Haven had shown up to search or provide food and beverages for the searchers.

Food. There had to be something left over from yesterday. She rummaged through the pantry and the fridge. There were cinnamon rolls and pastries she could serve for breakfast. Cam would need some eggs, too. She probably had some of that instant bacon. She usually had it on hand for emergencies.

Yup. She'd feed him and get rid of him. But how would she tell him she'd used him. There was no excuse for using him physically just because she'd been shaken and exhausted. Heck, she hadn't even known she was capable of such a thing. She'd been alone for so long she was used to dealing with everything alone, and now, she'd gone and dragged him into her life and had taken advantage of him to boot.

"Morning."

The plate of sweets she had in her hand clattered to the counter and cracked.

"Jeepers. You scared the crap out of me."

"Sorry." He sidled into the kitchen, shirtless, his unbuttoned jeans riding low on his hips.

Her mouth went dry, and she stared at him. Holy smokes. Her hormones thundered into overdrive. Her knees went weak. She wobbled on her feet.

"Let's try that again." He stepped up to her and drew her into his arms. Cupping her chin, he tipped her head and kissed her softly on the mouth. "Good morning, Lisa."

She stepped out of his arms. "Morning. Coffee?"

"Yes, please."

She turned and extracted two cups from the cupboard then set them carefully on the counter. She filled the mugs and placed them on the table. "I'll make some bacon and eggs for you."

"Lisa. Look at me."

She busied herself with the eggs, keeping her back to him. How could she look at him when she'd used him like that?

"Is this how it's going to be?" he asked quietly.

She closed her eyes and took a deep breath. "Last night was—"

"Don't even think about saying it was a mistake."

The touch of his hand on her shoulder made her jump. She cursed.

Gently, he turned her to face him. "Last night was not a mistake. It was something special between two consenting adults. Don't even think otherwise."

Blood rushed to her face, and she stared at the floor. God, he was so wrong.

"I apologize for last night," she whispered. "I was…out of sorts, and I used you. It won't happen again."

"You used me?" The anger in his voice snapped her gaze up to his face.

"Yes. I'm sorry."

"Hell, no."

"You don't have to accept my apology." Couldn't he be civil about this?

"I don't accept your apology because there's nothing to apologize for. You didn't use me. If anything, I took advantage of your distress. If anyone is going to apologize, it's me, and I have no intention of it."

"You better go." She turned away.

"I'm not leaving until we figure this out."

The calm certainty in his voice made her nerves twitch. What did he want?

"There's nothing to figure out. You said it yourself. Two consenting adults *consented* to have sex. End of story. Except, I used you for a distraction."

"Do you think I'm that stupid?"

She gaped at him. "No." Hell, he was anything but stupid. Not once had she thought that of him. A bit of a player, a total flirt, but not stupid. Never that.

"Then what are you driving at?"

"Look, Cameron. I was out of control last night, and I used you. I apologize."

"You said that already. There was nothing wrong or mistaken about last night. We were both sober. We'd both been through a very tough day. You needed comfort, and I offered it. Gladly. Last night was…"

"See, you don't even have words for it," she interrupted.

"Last night was special." He eased her into his embrace.

"I acted inappropriately."

"Jesus H. Christ. Lisa, listen to me. There was nothing inappropriate about last night. What is this? Is it your overdeveloped guilt gene, your upright morals, your fear? What? What makes you think you need to apologize, that either of us needs to?"

His arms were strong and gentle around her, his breathing even and calm.

"Can we just drop this? Pretend it never happened?" Her stomach clenched, and her shoulders went stiff. She'd known he was trouble from the first time she'd set eyes on him, but she sure hadn't realized he'd make her lose control like that.

His chest puffed out and stilled. He took several deep breaths, his body strong and solid against her. "No. We can't. Something changed between us last night. Our friendship is different. You… *we* have to accept that. I'd like to see more of you."

"Didn't you see enough last night?" She clapped a hand over her mouth.

He chuckled. "Hell, no. But that's not what I meant. I'd like to take you out again." He floundered. "Okay, not *again* because we've never dated. Damn, you've got me tongue-tied." He stepped away from her and paced the room.

She watched him warily, waiting for what he would say next.

"Lisa Marie Brown, I would like to take you on a date." He blushed.

"Cam…I'm not interested in a casual fling. Last night was an aberration."

"That's the weird thing. Last night wasn't casual. At least, not for me. You've become important to me. I like being around you. I adore Amy. I want to see where this crazy feeling goes."

She turned away and did some pacing of her own. What the heck was he thinking? They weren't compatible. They were nothing alike. He wasn't the kind of man she dated. He was too casual and irresponsible.

Okay, maybe not irresponsible. He was a partner in a successful business. And he'd stepped up to the plate when she'd needed him. He was wonderful with Amy. And even if she didn't want to admit it, he was kind and generous.

Good gravy. She wasn't considering this, was she?

"Okay." The word was out before she even knew she'd made a decision. She held up a hand, stopping his embrace. "But I'm not going to sleep with you again."

"What?"

"You heard me." Her heart pounded. He wouldn't push the issue, would he? She wasn't sure how she'd be able to resist him. She'd thrown herself at him last night and didn't want to do that again.

"Okay. I accept that." He kissed her on the forehead. "I'll pick you up at six for dinner."

"That's too soon to get a babysitter." It was the least of her objections, but the first she could easily articulate.

"You won't need one. We'll bring Amy. We'll have a picnic and play date at the park."

He kissed her again, leaving her breathless and wanting. "Six. Be ready." He winked and walked out of the kitchen. She followed him to the front door, her gaze glued to his backside. Dang, those jeans molded it to perfection. She inched up to him and patted it.

"Hey. No touching. This is strictly a platonic relationship." He winked at her groan. "Your rules…remember? Later, Pixie-Sticks."

He eased the door shut behind him.

She didn't know whether to laugh, cry or dance a jig. This would get complicated. She sighed, chuckled and went back to the kitchen. She really needed coffee. If she didn't get a jolt of caffeine soon, she'd lose her sanity altogether.

Promptly at six that evening, Cameron's truck pulled up in front of the house. Lisa peeked through the crack in the curtains as he jumped out and jogged up to the house. She waited a full minute after he knocked before she answered the door. No sense in letting him know how eagerly she'd anticipated his arrival.

"Cam," she said feigning surprise. "I didn't think you'd come." Guilt from the lie almost made her wince. She sucked at deception.

"Why wouldn't I?" he asked, tilting his head and squinting at her. "Have I ever broken my word to you?"

He hadn't, but she pretended to think over the question before responding. "No, I guess not. But I didn't necessarily expect you to follow through on a promise meant to placate me after sleeping with me."

"Did you need placating? Did you want me to skip out on dinner? What's going on, Lisa? I told you last night wasn't a mistake." He sighed heavily and closed his eyes for a second. When he opened them, he caught her gaze. "Give it up. I won't let you ruin this friendship. I don't know where it's going, but I'm asking you to give me, to give us, a chance to find out."

"I don't know…"

"What is it? What's bothering you?"

His voice was patient and understanding and knocked her breathless. Who was he? What happened to the Cameron who was hell-bent on a fling and nothing more?

"I don't get it. I don't get you," she offered helplessly. Her nerves were stretched bowstring tight. She wanted him, for more than a fling. Had he really changed, or was this some elaborate game she didn't know the rules to?

"Truth is…" He crossed his arms over his chest and rocked back and forth on his toes. "The truth is that I haven't the foggiest idea of what's going on. I'm confused. I'm uncertain. You make me feel things I've never felt before, and I don't know what the hell to do about." He grunted. "And now, I sound like a fricken girl. You're making me crazy."

His arms unfolded, and the right one shot out, grasped her behind the head and gently tugged her forward until she was only a fraction of an inch away from him. "You're messing with my head, and it's driving me crazy. But worse than that is the soul-crushing desire to kiss you." He leaned in slowly and brushed his lips gently across hers before backing away.

She stared up at him. His blue eyes shone, his pupils dilated, and his brows scrunched together. She reached up and smoothed the wrinkle between them. "Don't frown," she chided gently. His body tensed, and she dropped her hand.

"Okay, we'll need some ground rules, if we're going to see each other."

The frown left his face, replaced by a huge grin.

"Don't get your hopes up," she warned. "There are rules."

"Yes, ma'am. There are rules. Do I get to know what they are?"

She loved the laughter in his voice as he teased her, but more than that, she was impressed that he was willing to listen and play along.

"First, we keep Amy out of this. She's young, and she's already lost her father. I don't want her becoming attached to you."

"But—"

"No buts. You obey the rules, or you turn around and walk away right now."

She fixed him with her mom-stare, the one that demanded obedience. He nodded his acquiescence.

"Second, no sex." She almost laughed at the disappointed look on his face. Good, his needs might keep him interested, if she could keep hers in check. "Third, no kissing. Fourth, no showing up unannounced. Fifth, no telling anyone."

"Good grief, woman. This is Haven. Everybody knows everyone else's business before it even happens. How are we going to keep this a secret? Do we meet in secret, outside of town? What are you thinking?" He didn't wait for her response. "Wrong. There's no reasonable way to keep this a secret. It's unrealistic. It's not going to happen. But I'll be discreet."

She chuckled at the reality of his words. There were no secrets in Haven. "Okay, discretion over secrecy. I can deal with that."

"And I get one goodnight kiss after every date."

She wrinkled her nose and squinted at him. What was he up to?

"And one more thing, since you're so set on having rules. I pay for the babysitter. It comes out of my pocket, and I pay for everything on our dates."

"What?"

"Simple. We date; I pay. No discussion, no arguments."

"That's insane and totally archaically chauvinistic."

"Too bad. Take it or leave it."

She was sorely tempted to decline. But she wanted to know why first.

"Why?"

"Because I said so."

"That's not a reason, and only parents are allowed to use it." She planted her hands on her hips and visually demanded an explanation.

"Okay. Fine. Because you have a child to raise and can't afford extraneous expenditures. I've seen you at the grocery store price checking. I've seen you buy Amy a treat and deny yourself, even though you virtually drool every time you look at chocolate. I know you keep every light off to save power and you carefully water your flowers without waste. Be realistic, Lisa. You're a single mother on a tight budget. Let me do this. Let me treat you to some nice dinners and evenings out."

"I pay my own way. I'm not a scrounge, and I'm not taking your money. I'm not a gold-digger."

"I know that. That's why I offered—no, that's why I demand it."

"Chauvinist much?" She backed away and paced the length of the entryway.

"Call it what you will. If you get rules, I get rules. Every game has rules."

"You think this is a game?" She froze in her tracks and stared at him.

"Hell, no. Sorry. Heck, no. This is dead-on, drop-dead-serious business or pleasure or something. The only thing I'm sure of is that it's not a game." He slid his hands into his pocket and jingled his keys.

"Okay, I agree, with one stipulation."

"Rules? Stipulations? What's next? A contract drawn up by a lawyer?"

His eyes twinkled, and she knew he was teasing.

"Do you agree?"

"Heck no. Not until I hear what the stipulation is?" He laughed outright.

"Touché." She chuckled with him. "The stipulation is that at least half of our outings—"

"Dates," he corrected.

"Half of our…*outings* have to be ones that don't cost anything."

"You do know I have more than enough money to treat you well?" There was a hint of petulance in his voice.

"Don't know, don't care," she responded with a grin. "I'm not after your money, so find a way to entertain me without spending money."

"How the heck am I supposed to do that? You've already ruled out physical contact. Now, you add no spending money?"

"I have no intention of becoming accustomed to a lifestyle that requires money. I have a simple, inexpensive life and want to keep it that way. So, suck it up, and accept it."

"Can I ask a question?"

"You just did." She laughed at his surprise.

"Hardy-har-har. I'm laughing on the inside." He grinned. "Okay, on the outside, too. You've got a quick wit, and I like that." He stepped forward and dropped a kiss on her forehead.

"Hey, no kissing." She waggled her finger at him.

"The rules of engagement haven't been agreed on yet. Therefore, they don't apply."

She stuck her tongue out at him.

"You want rules and regulations? I'll give them to you." He made a so-there face.

"Are you going to ask that question or not?"

"Okay, Lisa. Let me ask you this. Do the rules allow me to cook for you at your house?"

"Am I expected to provide groceries?" The question puzzled her.

"No. I'll buy them."

"Then the answer is no. Groceries cost money, and the dates have to be free."

"That's unfair."

"How so?"

He scrubbed his hand through his hair thoughtfully. "Can I come inside? Or do I have to stand in the doorway all night?"

Lisa giggled. "Sorry, I forgot to ask you in. By all means, come in." She gestured widely for him to enter.

He took a step and paused. "Is Amy here? I don't want to violate the terms of my parole."

It took a second for the joke to penetrate.

"Parole? Goofball. You aren't on parole, and no, she isn't here. She's having a sleepover with Sasha. You won't be breaking any rules."

"Rules?" he quipped, stepping out of his shoes. "Laws. Dictates. Stipulations. Dating you is like living in a police state."

"Oh, you're just a laugh a minute." She chuckled and led him into the living room. "Would you like a glass of wine?"

"Beer?"

"Sorry, no beer. I have wine, water, juice, tea or coffee."

"Wine, please."

He followed her into the kitchen where she extracted a bottle of red wine from the refrigerator.

"Aren't you supposed to drink red wine at room temperature?"

"What are you? The wine police? I like it cold and with ice, so sue me." She opened the freezer and popped two ice cubes in her glass with a defiant look.

"Interesting…" He tapped his finger on his chin, feigning a thoughtful look. "A stickler for rules who breaks them at will. You're an enigma."

"Stuff it." She laughed and handed him the glass.

"So, back to the questions." He leaned against the counter and studied her.

His stare felt comfortable and arousing all at once. Her nipples pebbled under his glance, and she crossed her arms to cover the evidence. He gave her an I-saw-that look.

"So, if we were dating and I wasn't allowed to spend money, would you consider it fair for me to invite you to my house for dinner?"

"Where are you going with this?"

"Answer the question."

"I suppose it would be okay." She hesitated to give a firm answer.

"And since I live at Harmony's Bed and Breakfast and have no kitchen, wouldn't it be considered fair for me to cook for you, at your house, with food I provide?"

"I think you're grasping for a way to outmaneuver the rules."

"I think you're grasping for a way to make me obey unreasonable rules," he countered smugly.

"I am not."

"You are, too."

"Am not."

"Are, too."

They burst into laughter together.

"Clearly, we've regressed back into childhood," she quipped. "But I see your point. I'll allow you to cook for us, here, at your expense."

"Thank you. I appreciate it."

She sipped her wine and enjoyed the simple pleasure of looking at him. Gosh, he was handsome. Those sparkling, blue eyes and that rogue grin were enticing. She wanted to run her fingers through his hair. It was neat and clean, but just long enough to need a trim. It always seemed to be that length. Just on the unruly side of groomed. It suited him; close enough to the rules to say he followed them, but just enough outside to let you know he'd get his way. She almost laughed at how well his hair reflected his personality.

"What's the grin for?"

She chuckled. "You don't want to know. Come on. Let's sit in the living room and finish our wine."

"What about the picnic I promised you? I'd planned on taking you and Amy to the lake for a picnic."

"Honestly, and yes, honesty is another of my rules. Full disclosure of everything." She settled on the end of the couch, and he sat near her. Close enough to touch if she wanted to, but far enough away not to break any rules.

"I have no intention of lying to you about anything."

"I didn't think you did, but I wanted to be sure." She gulped her wine. "Honestly, I had a terrible day at work, and I really don't feel like going out. Can we reschedule?"

He looked thoughtfully at her. "How about a compromise? We stay in and have the picnic here, on the couch? I can't take the food back to the store; I have no fridge at the B&B, so let's keep it casual and eat here instead of going to the lake."

"I can live with that."

"Wow, don't overdo the enthusiasm," he teased. "Wait here. I'll be back in a jiffy with our dinner."

CHAPTER 28

Less than two minutes later, Cameron knocked lightly on the door then let himself back into the house.

"Don't get up," he called. "I've got this. You relax, and I'll prepare our feast. Well, not exactly a feast, but supper anyway."

Back in the living room, he discovered Lisa hadn't moved an inch since he'd left. He set the cardboard box and picnic basket he'd carried in from his truck on the floor and moved the coffee table out of the way, leaving the whole area between the couch and the television empty.

He smiled at her. "You look exhausted."

"Gee, thanks."

He felt his face flush. Why did he keep making simple errors with her? He never made them with any of his other female friends. He usually considered his words before he spoke them.

"I didn't mean you look bad, just that I can see you're tired. Were you run off your feet at work?"

"No, not really. One of the cooks was sick, so the wait for food was longer than usual, and that makes people grumpy. Grumpy customers don't tip, and well, you know how it goes."

"Well, I've never been a waitress, but I dated someone once

who thought waiters were the lowest form of life and treated them poorly. I spent a ton of money on tips and apologized to a lot of servers to compensate for her crappy behavior." He shrugged.

"But isn't that the measure of a person? You can tell a lot about who a person really is by how they treat people who can give them nothing?"

"I realized that one day. Shortly after, she and I broke up. In retrospect, I'm not even sure why I dated her for so long. I haven't dated anyone with that attitude since. Common courtesy and respect go a long way." He pulled a blanket from the box he'd brought in.

"What are you doing?"

He paused, mid-motion. "Spreading this picnic blanket on the floor?"

She snorted. "I can see that. I meant why?"

"Pixie-Sticks, you are beyond tired if you can't figure it out. We're having a picnic…hence the blanket." He smoothed the edges of it with his feet then extracted a portable speaker from the box. He set it aside, flipped the box over then covered it with a white cloth. "Your table," he said for clarification and began setting out containers of food.

"Tonight's menu includes macaroni and cheese, bologna, cheese, crackers, pickles, carrot sticks, marshmallows, chocolate, orange slices, toddler stars—whatever those are—apple juice and dessert."

"That's a feast fit for—"

"For a four-year-old." He chuckled. "I know, I was planning on impressing Amy. I thought by impressing her, I'd impress you." He plugged his cell phone into the speaker. "Although, I think I'll change my music selection." He started scrolling through the music folders on his phone.

"Oh no, you don't. This I've got to hear." She laughed and slid off the couch to sit on the floor beside his makeshift table.

"I don't think so," he demurred.

"Cameron…"

"Oh crap, she's breaking out my full name, just like my grand-mother used to when I'd messed up. This is bad." He raised one hand in mock surrender. "Okay, but remember, you asked for it." He touched the screen, and Disney music flowed from the speaker.

"Okay, enough." She laughed. "You win. Put on some grown-up music."

"But I downloaded the music from five Disney princess movies…"

"Wow, you really were trying to impress. But if it's okay with you, I'd prefer something less princess, something more grown up."

The low, introductory tones of an instrumental tune flowed from the speakers.

"Oh, big band music. I love swing."

"Hey, me, too. It's soothing and entertaining and not distract-ing." He settled beside her and handed her a plate and napkin. "I wish now that I'd put more thought into what you wanted, rather than what would please Amy." He handed her an insulated casserole dish of macaroni.

Her soft smile stole his breath and sent his heart galloping.

"Funny thing is," she replied, "by trying to please Amy, you've pleased me." She leaned over and kissed his cheek.

Unbidden, his hand rose and cupped her cheek. Sliding his fingers into her short hair, he eased her forward and touched his lips to hers. Kissing her was like heaven. He wanted to deepen the kiss, to taste all of her. Instead, he dropped his hand and backed off.

"Sorry. I forgot the rules. No kissing."

"I'll let it go, this one time." She pecked his cheek again. "You deserve it for trying to make this picnic special for Amy."

"I'm glad I pleased you. Now, eat up so I can get you in bed."

Her eyes widened in surprise.

"Not like that!" He pretended he hadn't meant the double entendre. "Eat up then hit your bed. I'll go home…alone." He made sure his voice was plaintive. "You need some rest. You're exhausted."

"Are you playing me?" She flashed him a quizzical look.

"Playing you?" he inquired. "Why would you think that?"

She didn't answer, so he mentally reran their conversation in his head. "Okay, I can see where you might get that, but I'm not. I told you ages ago that I don't play that kind of game. What you see is what you get."

"I doubt that," she replied, verbalizing her concern. "I think there's a lot to you that you keep hidden, which makes that statement a prevarication at best or an outright lie at worst. I'm going to let it go, this time, but honesty is a requirement in this relationship. If you aren't going to be honest, you'd better go."

"You realize you've cut me a break twice in the last five minutes? Right?"

"Yes."

"Why?" He pivoted so he faced her directly. "You set the rules; I break them then you let it go. It's inconsistent."

She sighed heavily. "Okay, I was hoping you wouldn't notice." She kept her glance from meeting his and stared at her knees.

"Look at me, please, Lisa." He stared at the top of her head, willing her to look up at him. "Come on, Lisa. What's up?"

She was weirding him out. First, she was all schoolmarm and mother; then, all choir girl and honesty; and now, she was hiding things. What was going on inside that pretty head?

"Please?" he repeated.

Finally, she exhaled a long, slow breath and raised her head.

"What's going on with you? You're sending mixed signals." A thousand questions rattled through his head, and he couldn't settle on the right one, so he simply said, "Talk to me."

CHAPTER 29

What was with him? He kept pushing her. He kept making her test her boundaries. She didn't want to acknowledge her inconsistency.

"Okay, it's like this." She raised her head and looked him in the eye. "I'm not usually inconsistent. I choose my path and stick to it. I'm not saying I never change my mind. But you make me crazy. I want you around; I don't want you around." She wrapped her arms around her waist and glanced away. "Cameron Zeus, you make me want things I can't have, things you can't give me. You told me you couldn't, and I accepted that. But after we… After last night—"

"After we made love?" he interrupted.

"After we had sex," she clarified defiantly. "After that, I wanted more. I see good things in you. I see the man you could be but won't let yourself be. You're running from something, and I want to know what it is."

"I'm not running from anything. I'm here, aren't I?"

"Physically, yes. But mentally and emotionally? I don't think you are. You're still hiding, and that bothers me." She took a deep breath. Setting down her plate, she stood and paced the small confines of the room. "I want to accept what you offer. I want to see where this goes, if it goes anywhere. But it isn't enough for me. I need it all. I need the entire Cameron Zeus. I need your past, your present and your future." She waved a hand to forestall his words when he opened his mouth to respond.

After a few seconds of introspection, she went on. "Look, I can't ask for what I want. That's not who I am. I try to accept everyone for who they are, but my attraction to you is pushing me. It's driving me to dig deeper. That need to know more is why I keep cutting you breaks when normally I'd walk away."

She studied him. His face was completely devoid of expression. It revealed absolutely nothing about his thoughts. The rigid set of his shoulders and the clenching and unclenching of his hands told her she'd made him uncomfortable, maybe even mad, but he was trying hard not to reveal anything.

What was going on inside of his head? She should never have agreed to this picnic, with or without Amy. It started her down a road she didn't want to travel. From the first moment when he'd stood up for her at the café, there had been something about him, something strong and worthy hidden behind his mask of casual bravado and easy camaraderie.

As their friendship had grown, she couldn't help but think he wanted more than just a fling. Did his desire for more lay buried so deep he didn't recognize it?

He kept coming around, helping out and being strong for her. He'd been her rock when Amy had disappeared. He attributed it to friendship, but it didn't feel like friendship. It certainly wasn't the same friendship she shared with Clint. Or Nick. Or any of the other men she was friends with.

She felt an emotional intimacy and vulnerability with Cameron she didn't experience with anyone else, and it was unnerving. She flopped down on the couch and looked at him. He hadn't said anything, offering no response to her ramblings.

"I don't know, Cameron. I'm confused and uncertain, and I

don't know how to take you sometimes. Even my feelings are unclear. Maybe you'd better go. I need time to think."

"How about a compromise?" he asked after a long pause. "We could watch a movie and be here, as friends, while we finish our picnic. No deep conversations, no probing questions. Just two people having dinner together."

She opened her mouth to refuse him, but the words wouldn't come. He looked too hopeful. "Fine."

"Fine?" he asked. "Don't sound so enthusiastic." He started putting away the food.

"No, wait. I didn't mean it like that. Stay. We'll finish dinner and watch something. I agreed to this picnic, and I'll stick to my word."

"That doesn't sound much better." He chuckled. "But it sounds honest. I promise to be on my best behavior. You're an enigma, Lisa Marie Brown, and I want to unravel that complexity and lay it out straight so I can understand it. The truth of the matter is, for the first time ever, I want to follow a relationship, this relationship, and see what happens. I know that isn't enough for you, but I'm asking for the chance to get to know you better."

She watched as he perched on the edge of the couch beside her. His expression was wary and hopeful, and it was her undoing. She patted the seat beside her. "Pass me my wine and take a seat."

The wide smile that wreathed his face and lit up his blue eyes was thanks enough. That's when she realized how important his happiness was to her.

Yup, she was doomed.

Cameron parked his truck on a quiet, residential street in Southwest Calgary. He strode up the walk to the two-story house his sister, Angela, shared with her husband and children. Bright green with white gingerbread trim, it had a happy, homey feel. He pounded on the door.

Her husband, Jefferson, opened it. "Jesus, dude. No need to knock it down. What the hell are you doing here? You didn't even call." He yanked Cam into his arms for a man-hug.

"I need to talk to Ang." They strolled into the kitchen.

"She's at soccer with Travis. They'll be back any minute. I just go home from work. Wanna beer?"

"Hell, yeah."

"What brings you back to Calgary? I thought you were living in the sticks." Jefferson gave him the manly stink-eye. He twisted the tops off two bottles of beer and handed Cam one.

"Thanks. Hey, guy code. No questions. Remember?"

"Fuck that shit. You show up unannounced looking for Ang. That means girl trouble. It always has. Sit." He gestured through an arched doorway to the family room.

"I love this room," Cam said, flopping onto the couch. He

looked around. Toys, dolls, cars and blocks were scattered every-where. Children's art and photographs covered the walls. It was a pigsty. No, that wasn't accurate. It was messy and lived in, but it was clean. There were no dirty dishes, no dust and no garbage. Just a shit-ton of kid toys everywhere.

"You never answered the question. What's up?"

At that moment, the front door opened, and the kids rushed in, followed by Angela and the baby. Save by the bell.

"I knew that was your truck, Unka Cam," four-year-old Travis blurted, throwing himself onto Cam's lap.

"Dude. Watch the junk," he teased his nephew. "I might need that."

Seven-year-old Randy flopped down beside them.

Ang strolled over, kissed him on the cheek and dumped Moxie on his lap. "Yo, bro. What's happening?"

"Girl trouble," Jefferson declared with a laugh.

"That would make sense." Ang laughed. "Holidays and girl trouble are the only things that bring him here."

"That's not true," Cam blurted.

Angela and Jefferson laughed aloud.

"Hey, give a guy a break. Can't I want to see my sister?"

"No." Angela laughed again. "Watch the kids. I'll make dinner. And then we'll talk." She gave him the mom-eye and disappeared into the kitchen. From beyond the doorway, Cam heard her call out, "Does Mom know you're here?"

"No! And don't you go calling her, either."

"I can't believe you haven't reconciled with her yet," Jefferson nagged.

"Drop it. That day may never come."

"She's mellowed. She's not as selfish as she used to be. She's great with the kids."

"I said drop it." Moxie crawled off Cam's lap and grabbing his finger, encouraging him to join her on the floor beside a pile of blocks.

He stacked them up so she could knock them down. Laughing and giggling, she helped him create a wobbly stack and knocked it down again. The game continued until they were called to eat.

Dinner was a raucous, boisterous affair with bickering, laughing and teasing. Eventually, the kids were sent off to bed, and the adults settled down for a glass of wine. Angela snuggled against Jefferson's side on the couch, and Cam sat across from them in a wide, cushiony chair.

"Sorry about the noise," Angela apologized.

"No worries. I love it." Cam waved off her apology.

"When are you having kids of your own?" she pushed.

Jefferson laughed at Cam's scowl. Angela ignored it.

"How did you know?" Cam asked point blank.

"Know what?" they asked in unison, smirking at each other.

"How do you know when you're in love?" he asked.

"You should know. You were engaged. Why?"

"I thought I loved Kim. Now, I'm not so sure I did. And I wondered…"

"Are you getting serious about someone?" Ang asked, dropping all pretense of amusement.

"No. Yes. Maybe," he stammered. How did you explain that you had no idea what you felt, what you wanted? Despite his tumultuous upbringing and engagement, or maybe because of them, he couldn't put a finger on his feelings. This emotional shit was chick territory, not a guy thing. That's why he'd come to see his sister.

"Tell us about her." Angela's voice held no pressure, no judgment, just encouragement. "Where did you meet her?"

"Her name is Lisa. She's slender, beautiful, and she looks like a pixie. She's got a great sense of humor, killer legs and is smart."

"Is she hot?" Jefferson grunted when his wife smacked him in the stomach for the rude question.

"Hell, yeah. But…" He could see they were waiting to see what came next. He struggled to find the right words. "But she's got a kid."

"And?"

Leave it to Ang to get right to the point. She'd always been like that. Pushing the right, or was it wrong, buttons?

"She doesn't want what I want."

"And that is?"

"She wants happily-ever-after, and I don't do that shit. Happy endings are a Hollywood lie. They're bullshit. Look at Mom and Dad. Me and Kim. Love is a lie."

"So that's what's got you so tied in knots? Mom and Dad and that bitch you were engaged to? That wasn't love. Mom never loved Dad. They got married because Mom was pregnant with me after a drunken, one-night stand."

"What the fuck? How did I not know that?"

"Come on, bro. You disappeared right out of high school. You couldn't get gone fast enough. Dad didn't believe in divorce, and Mom hated his guts. It drove him to drink. It made them both miserable."

Wow. Holy fuck. Had he really been that oblivious to what had been going on around him? The whole idea was crazy, but it made sense. It cleared up a thousand mistaken ideas from his childhood.

"And you know Kim just used you for a meal ticket until Mr. Right came along. Didn't you?"

"Not until she dumped me. I thought I was in love with that bitch."

"Dude, you spent more time avoiding her than being with her," Jefferson chipped in helpfully.

"Don't remind me."

"And now, you've met Lisa. Is that her name?"

He nodded.

"And you don't know what you feel." Sympathy filled Angela's voice.

"Have you slept with her?"

"Jeepers, Jefferson. What kind of question is that?" Angela glared at her husband.

"None of your damn business," Cam snapped. Who did he think he was asking questions like that? Questioning Lisa's morality? As if he'd tell them anyway.

Then it hit him. Jesus. Fuck. He was in love with Lisa.

Holy freaking hand grenades.

"Well, fuck."

Angela burst into laughter. "You love her. Well hala-fricken-looya. The love bug has finally bit my slut brother. No more tomcatting around for you."

Slut? His sister thought he was a man-slut? Shame filled him. He'd never treated women like that. He'd respected them all. Recognition dawned. From the outside, it would look like he whored around. Fuck. He was an asshole.

"Give him a break. Love isn't easy for guys. How long did it take you to convince me we were meant to be together?"

"Good point." She laughed and kissed Jefferson on the cheek. "And I'm glad I stuck with it. I love you." She turned back toward Cam. "So, what are you going to do?"

"Jesus, how do women do that, that mom-stare thing?"

"She's mastered the mom-stare?" Angela laughed. "You have to be a mom to learn that. So, tell us about her child."

"She has a four-year-old girl. Amy. She's adorable. Rotten to the core some days, but sweet as honey the rest."

"How does her ex feel about you hanging around?"

"He doesn't. She's a widow."

"Oh, you know what they say about widows?" Jefferson chuckled lewdly then grunted when Angela jabbed him in the stomach with her elbow.

"Don't go there." Cam's fists bunched, and he fought the urge to leap out of his chair. "She isn't like that. Not at all. She's a good woman and a great mom. You'd like her, Ang."

"I can't wait to meet her. When are you bringing them to visit?"

She'd cold-cocked him again with her simple question. Would he take this to the next level? Would he get serious? Did he want to get serious?

Questions swirled around his head, colliding and creating new questions. It felt as if his head would explode. Without an example to follow, he had no idea how this love thing worked. Nor did he know what he wanted or needed to do next.

"How do I know if I love her?" he finally blurted.

"Do you miss her when you don't see her? Is her happiness more important than yours? Do you want to do things for her, to help her out? Do you want to know everything about her and meet her family? Is she stuck in your mind at night and when you wake up in the morning?"

She rattled off a half-dozen more questions, without waiting for answers. He'd be damned if he didn't mentally answer yes to all of them.

Well, he'd be gob-smacked. He did love Lisa.

What the hell did he do now?

"I don't even know what to do," he blurted in a fit of panic.

"Do?"

"I don't know how to be in love." Blood thundered in his head, and his heart pounded as if it would burst from his chest. "I don't know anyone who's in love."

Angela burst into laughter. "Idiot. Me? Jefferson? Sterling and Grace? You must have more friends who are in relationships or married. Do what they do."

"Walk around in a love-sick daze? Get all goo-goo eyed? Hell no!"

This time, Jefferson laughed. "Dude, if you love her, you'll want to put her first and spend time with her. It won't matter what you're doing, as long as you're with her. Treat her nice. Do nice things for her. Bring her flowers. Treat her like you treated everyone you've dated, only know that it might last a long time. It isn't complicated if you're in love."

"But I thought I loved Kim…"

"You never loved Kim. She was comfortable and took the pressure off dating." Angela left the couch and walked over to him. She hugged him tightly and kissed his cheek. "Come on, bro. Man up. Think about it. Love's not easy. Sometimes, it's a bitch. But if she's worth it, you'll know and you'll fight for it…for her. Get some sleep. The spare room in the basement is made up. I'll see you in the morning." She kissed him again. "Come on, husband. Let's hit the hay."

They disappeared upstairs, leaving Cam thinking about everything they'd said.

CHAPTER 31

Cam sat in his truck in front of Lisa's house. A light shone in the living room, despite the late hour. She must still be awake. He should just go talk to her. He wanted—no, *needed*—to see her. But he felt frozen from the inside. Dear God, how did a man dredge up the courage to talk to a woman about something serious? He'd never been in this position, and frankly, he was scared shitless. Not once in his entire life had he felt on edge like this. Panic flashed through him. What if he was wrong? What if she didn't like him?

Before today, self-confidence had never been an issue. He'd been called the cock-of-the-walk more than once. So why couldn't he dredge up the balls to get out of the truck? Leaning his elbow on the steering wheel, he covered his face with his hands. He raked his hands through his hair, barely resisting the urge to pull it out. What the hell was he going to do? Leave? Yeah! That was it. He'd leave and forget he'd ever come here to talk to her.

Fuck.

Leaving didn't feel any safer than getting out of the truck. Damn. He was a wimp. Who'd have ever thought Cameron Zeus, named after a god, would turn out to be a chicken-shit? Sterling would have a field day with this. Cam dropped his head to the steering wheel and closed his eyes, searching for courage. He felt like the cowardly lion.

The passenger door of his truck popped open.

He bolted upright.

"Cameron? Are you okay?"

"Lisa? Shit," he blurted, without thinking.

"Are you okay? You've been sitting out here for twenty minutes." She reached across the seat and touched his arm compassionately. "Do I need to phone an ambulance?"

Well, this was going like shit. So much for being a man and opening up to her about his feelings. He sighed.

"I'm fine. I was just… I was thinking." Great, now he sounded like a moron. This just got better and better. "I need a drink."

"I have wine and whiskey," she offered. "Come inside."

Crap, he'd said that aloud. Shit balls. What was the line that Ryan guy had used in that vampire movie? *Fuck. Fuck me sideways.* Perfect words for a shitty situation.

"Cam?" Her voice vibrated with worry.

Next, she'd be giving him the mom-eye.

"I'm fine." He undid his seatbelt and climbed out of the truck. "I'll take that wine." He wanted whiskey but couldn't risk losing his head.

He rounded the truck and headed for the sidewalk. She wrapped her arm around his waist and hugged him tight, as if she were prepared to support him. It was obvious she cared. Why did this freak him out so badly?

"Come inside," she whispered. "I'll fix us a drink, and we'll talk about whatever's eating you up. I can see the stress. It's practically radiating off you. You look like a bomb that's about to go off. I've never seen you like this, but I'll help you work through it. Whatever it is. Okay?"

They settled on the couch, side by side, with glasses of wine close at hand. He picked his up and downed it one smooth move. "More, please."

"Wow. You are rattled." She filled his glass. "Take your time. I'm ready to listen when you're ready to talk. I've got all night."

Her calm words reassured him. She really was one of the good ones. Stable. Caring. Compassionate. She had it all. Even beauty.

"I don't know where to start." He sighed and set his glass on the table.

"How about the beginning?"

He chuckled. "That's so perfectly you. Just like a mom. You always know the right words."

"Heck, no. I never know the right words. But Mom always told me to do my best and say what I felt but to think twice in case it hurt someone's feelings."

"This shouldn't hurt." He paused. "I think."

He didn't look at her. He couldn't. Seeing her face would scare him, but he had no choice. He had to get the words out. Jesus. This should be easy. It shouldn't be this hard. The beginning. She'd said start at the beginning.

"When I was a kid, my dad was a drunk. A mean drunk. And my mom is a self-centered bit—" He floundered. "She was self-centered. I didn't know why until yesterday. Last night, that is." He puffed out a breath, battling for calm. "I went to visit Ang and Jefferson and the rats."

"I'll bet that was nice. Family can be calming. Or not." She laughed. "Sometimes, they drive you bat-crap crazy."

"Not this time. I went because I had something on my mind." He twisted his hands together.

"Okay." The simple word was both acceptance and encouragement for him.

"I've been twisted up in knots about some shi—er, crap. So, I went to talk to Ang. She told me something. Something I'd had no idea about. I can't figure out how I was so blind to it. But I left home like a bat out of hell right after graduation and never really went back. I missed the blatantly obvious." He sipped his wine, swallowing hard. "I never understood why my parents got married. It was obvious from the time I was small that they hated each other. Dad took that out on all of us. Ang told me why."

He closed his eyes, searching for calm. It was embarrassing that he'd been so wrapped up in his life that he'd missed the obvious with his parents.

"I just thought they were self-centered. Ang told me they'd gotten married young because Mom was pregnant. They'd hoped to make it work, but they couldn't. They were never happy, but Dad didn't believe in divorce. Instead, he punished us all, even himself, for their miserable marriage. That agony, that hatred, soured me on relationships."

"But you've had a lot of relationships?" Her words were both a statement and a question.

"Yes. No. Sort of. Damn. This is difficult." He leapt up and paced across the room. Pulling back the drapes, he looked outside. "I dated a lot. More than my fair share. Hell, I dated so much I can't even guess at numbers and sure as hell can't remember all their names. But none of them were real relationships. Some of them turned into friendships, but none of them could be classified as serious. Hell, most of them were flings."

"I knew that." There was no judgment in her voice, just compassion.

"I was a man-slut."

She laughed at that. "O-kay."

"I mean it. I didn't see it, but looking back, all I did was whore around. I never even tried to get to know them. Not a single one of them. At least, not until you. With you, I didn't have a choice. You were just always there, popping up when I didn't expect it. You knew my dating habits but never treated me badly for it. I don't understand why."

"Is that what this is all about? I messed with your head because I respected you?"

"Yes. No." He turned back to her.

She had a small grin, but not a malicious one. She just looked…pleased. "I believe people can change. I believe our pasts shapes us, but don't define who we are or what we'll become. I see good in you, Cameron Zeus. You're a good man. If you weren't, you'd never have gotten close to Amy and me. I let you in because I saw who you are, who you are deep down."

"I think that's why I liked you."

"Liked?" Her tone was wary.

"Like." He took a deep breath and returned to sit beside her. "Don't distract me. I've got more to say." He reached for his glass, and she stilled his hand with hers.

"Is it that bad that you have to be drunk to tell me? Are you sure you're ready?"

He leaned in and kissed her gently on the cheek. "You're so compassionate. So good. A glass and a half of wine won't make me drunk."

She nodded and dropped her hand.

He took a small sip.

"I was engaged once," he blurted.

"I thought so. You mentioned your ex once or twice."

"I didn't love her. I thought I did."

"And?"

"She was comfortable. Easy to be with, at first. But looking back, I didn't love her, and she didn't love me. I think I was Mr. Right-Now for her. Not Mr. Right. We dated. Somehow, we got engaged because it was comfortable and easy. I didn't know she was waiting for Mr. Perfect. She found him, and I caught her sleeping with him, in our bed." His breath shuddered out. "Fuck. This is hard. She told me she didn't love me, that she could never love a laborer. Turns out the guy owned half the city. He's rich as fuck. They're married. I don't know if they're happy. Hell, I don't care. I was just glad to see the ass end of her."

"That must have hurt." She leaned against him, wrapping her arm around his waist.

She was so warm, so soft, so compassionate, that his fears fled.

"Here's the thing." He pivoted to face her and took her hands in his. "I've been a jackass. A colossal ass-hat. I've been a jerk and treated you badly. I chased you even while I was running away from you. I couldn't stay away. Somehow, between meeting you in the café and when Amy went missing, I fell in love with you. The last few weeks, while we've been dating, have been incredible for me."

"Oh my," she whispered.

"You're a wonderful woman. You make me happy. You saw who I was and accepted that. I treated you with disrespect, and you didn't deserve that. But I'll be damned if I can stay away."

"You never disrespected me."

He looked at her with one eyebrow raised.

"Okay, maybe once, when you implied I was a horny widow."

"And other times, too. God, I slept with you the day Amy disappeared. I took advantage of your distress and slept with you."

She laughed outright at that one. "Cam, you've got that one so backward it isn't even funny. I was shaken and scared and emotional. And I took what I wanted from you. I needed your touch, your warmth and your compassion to get over my shock. You gave that to me willingly. Eagerly. You gave me what I asked for. I knew you liked me, as a friend at least, and I took advantage of your attraction. I used you to steady myself. If anyone was wrong there, it was me. I was already in love with you. I didn't want to be, but I was. I took advantage of your attraction to take a piece of you, knowing I'd never have all of you."

He gaped at her.

"Close your mouth, Cam. I'm not perfect. Not by any stretch. Do you know how many hours I've bemoaned the fact I used you? Dozens, maybe more. You were there for me, and I used you." She blushed and looked down.

"Hey. Don't be ashamed of your passion." He cupped her chin

in his hand and turned her face up, encouraging her to meet his eyes. "I didn't know it then—okay, I *did* know it, but I didn't want to admit it—but I loved you then. I wasn't having sex with you. I wasn't using you. I was making love to you. Because I love you."

He dropped his forehead to hers and sucked in a couple deep breaths. She was shaking. Jesus. He'd hurt her. She was crying. Crap on toast. He looked up.

She wasn't crying. She was laughing.

"You're laughing at me?" he blurted.

"I'm laughing at us," she corrected and kissed him long and slow and deep, pouring every ounce of emotion and love she felt into the kiss.

He felt the love in that kiss and in her hands as she drew him closer.

"At us?" he asked when she eased the kiss to an end.

"At us. What a couple of goofballs we are. I don't know when I fell in love with you. Lord knows it was lust at first sight. But I couldn't risk my heart. I didn't know I'd risked it anyway until you made love to me. But after? Then I knew it was too late. And you?" She chuckled again. "You were so busy running away from me that you ran right into me."

He chuckled with her. She was right. They'd both been so busy avoiding a relationship that they'd developed a friendship that had turned into something more.

"You, Cameron Zeus, are a good man. You've got a loving heart. You're kind and compassionate, and I fell in love with you despite myself. I love you, Cameron."

He dropped to his knees in front of her. He banked down the urge to laugh at her wary expression, but he couldn't let this moment pass, despite being unprepared for it. He took her hands in his and looked her in the eye. He swallowed hard. *Here goes nothing.*

"Lisa Marie Brown, will you do me the honor of becoming my wife? I don't think I can live without you for another day. You're my heart, and I swear you're half of my soul." His heart pounded until it was a dull roar in his ears, blocking out everything else.

She studied him long and hard, worrying her lip with her teeth.

Oh, fuck. She was going to say no! He closed his eyes. God, this was so embarrassing.

"Yes."

"What?" His eyes popped open, and he stared at her. "What?"

"Yes." She threw her arms around him and kissed him senseless. "Yes, I'll marry you. I love you."

"Oh, thank fuck. I thought you were going to say no." He collapsed against her in relief.

She laughed then, and he joined her.

"God, I thought you were going to rip out my heart. I'm such a pussy," he groaned.

She laughed again. "You're not a pussy. Much. You're just not used to having a heart; that's all. And you'll have to learn to watch that mouth around Amy," she teased.

"I'll try. I swear I'll try my best to do right by her."

Lisa's soft smile of acceptance warmed his heart.

"I don't have a ring for you. I thought you might like to choose it yourself." He blushed. "Okay, I wasn't going to propose yet, just let you know I was ready to get serious." He shrugged off his embarrassment. "But the time seemed right."

She drew him closer and kissed him. "I accept anyway, and we can pick something together. You might not have brought a ring, but that's okay. You have other redeeming features." She waggled her eyebrows at him.

"Such as?"

"Come to the bedroom, and let this horny widow show you a thing or two."

"Are you ever going to let me live that down?" he groaned.

"Never." She led him down the hallway to her bedroom.

CHAPTER 32

"Come on, girl. Let's do this." Grace kissed Lisa on the cheek. "Let's get this wedding over with and get the party started."

They laughed together.

"I'm so nervous. What if he changes his mind?"

"He's not going to change his mind," Natalie teased. "Look at him. He looks impatient, not scared."

Lisa peeked through the doors to Haven's church sanctuary. Bright bunches of sunflowers and daisies lined the pews, each bunch wrapped in rich green ribbon. They matched her bouquet of a single sunflower surrounded by a halo of daisies and wrapped in green and white ribbon. Not a traditional bouquet, but one she loved. The church was packed. The entire town must be here. People were lined up along the walls, and it was standing room only. There was nothing like a wedding to draw in a crowd.

Cam stood at the front beside Haven's new minister, Jebediah Crowley. Jeb had replaced the retiring minister two months ago after three months of on-the-job training. Sterling, Nick and Clint were there as best man and groomsmen. They made a stunning vista in their black suits with dark green cummerbunds. They were all fit and handsome. But Cam, dang, he was drool-worthy. Love flooded her heart. How had she ever managed to convert such a lady's man into a potential husband when she hadn't even been trying? Natalie was right. He didn't look nervous. He looked… happy and impatient. What a funny combination.

Lisa studied her bridesmaids. Grace and Natalie looked stunning. So did Belinda. New to town, Belinda had quickly become a fast and true friend; and since Cam insisted on three groomsmen, Lisa had invited Belinda to be a bridesmaid.

"Okay. Let's do this." Lisa shut the door and leaned down to kiss Amy. "You ready, kiddo? Just walk up the aisle after Grace, Natalie and Belinda. Walk up slowly and sprinkle the flower petals as you go. Can you do that for me?"

"Is Cam really gonna be my new daddy?"

"He really is."

They'd discussed this a dozen times over the last month. Wasn't it just like a kid to pick a rotten time to ask questions she already knew the answer to?

"Is he gonna go to heaven like my old daddy?"

"Not for a very long time."

"Good, 'cause I loves him."

Lisa chuckled. One disaster averted. The last thing she needed on her wedding day was to deal with a temper tantrum. "And he loves you. When it's your turn, you walk to the front and stand beside him."

"'Kay."

The wedding march started. She embraced her daughter then her friends and whispered, "Let's do this."

One of the church ladies opened the door, and Grace strode through, followed by Natalie then Belinda. Lisa nodded at Amy, who headed out after them, her pace faster than it should be, as if she was eager to have her job finished. She hopped onto the dais beside Cam and tugged on his sleeve.

"Mr. Cameron, Mom says you're my new daddy."

The crowd chuckled, and Lisa froze in the doorway.

Kids!

CAM KNELT and looked Amy in the eye. "I am going to be your new daddy, if it's okay with you. I love you very much."

She wrapped her arms around his shoulders and kissed him solemnly on the cheek. "I love you, too." She rested her head on his shoulder.

He rose with Amy in his arms.

"Look. There's Mommy. Isn't she beautiful?" He stared down the aisle, looking rather love-struck. She took his breath away. She'd opted against a veil, and her hair was spiked in its usual pixie fashion, and unless he missed his guess, it had glitter in it. It sparkled in the dim light of the church. Her dress was a narrow sheath, clinging gently to her curves and widening at the bottom like a tall, narrow bell. It shimmered with each step she took. It was perfect, light, fanciful and so completely Lisa.

"How did I get so lucky to marry you both?"

"I'm getting married," Amy whooped, making the crowd laugh.

TEARS BRIMMED in Lisa's eyes. Cameron wasn't the lucky one. She was. This consummate bachelor had turned into a patient, dedicated, family man who loved her and adored her daughter. Life just didn't get any better.

"Hurry, Mommy. We has to get married."

The crowd laughed again, and Lisa quickened her steps.

She stepped up on the small dais beside her friends and family and took her place. They turned to face the crowd and the minister. Cam leaned over and kissed her on the cheek.

"Ahem." Jeb cleared his throat. "Let's save the kissing until after the vows."

Cam blushed. "Okay. Sorry." He winked at Lisa and stood there beside her, Amy in his arms.

"Ladies and gentlemen, friends and family, we are gathered here together in the sight of God to join this couple…"

The ceremony was short, sweet and traditional and seemed to last an eternity, even as it flew by. At last, Jeb pronounced them man and wife.

Drawing Lisa into his one-armed embrace, Cam kissed her thoroughly then gave Amy a peck on the cheek before setting her down to stand between them.

They walked back down the aisle, holding hands with Amy between them, to the cheers of all of Haven.

Did you enjoy this book?
If you did, please consider leaving a review on the platform of your choice.
Reviews are an author's life blood.

ABOUT KATIE O'CONNOR

Katie O'Connor lives in Calgary, Alberta, Canada. She married her high school sweetheart and is living her happily ever after. She is the mother of two grown daughters and is extremely proud of her five grandchildren. She has two wonderful sons-in-law and a large support network of friends, family and fellow authors.

Katie's career path has been long and twisted, with most of her life devoted to her family. She's been a waitress, chambermaid, cashier, store manager, as well as a lab and x-ray technician. She is an avid quilter and crafter.

She's dabbled in writing since high school because something drives her to create stories. She swears that it's impossible for her NOT to write. Unsatisfied with one genre, Katie writes contemporary romance, erotic romance and erotica. Recently, she's crafted her first cozy mystery with the intention of publishing a cozy mystery series.

She believes in all things magical; including dragons, fairies, UFOs, ghosts, and house pixies. But most of all she believes in love, romance and hope.

Katie likes to make it up as she goes along and dreams of publishing a mixed genre novel. It is going to be an erotic, shape shifter, vampire, steampunk, sci-fi, murder mystery, adventure, romantic, western, historical, thriller. It will be her biography.

CONTACT KATIE O'CONNOR

Katie loves to hear from her readers. Feel free to contact her anytime.

Website: https://katieohwrites.com
Email: katie@katieohwrites.com
Facebook: http://www.facebook.com/katieohwrites

Reviews are an author's life blood.

To thank readers generous enough to leave a review, I hold a monthly draw for a free e-book. To enter, simply email me the link to your review. (katie@katieohwrites.com)
Each month's winner will receive the e-book of their choice from Katie's publications.

Thank you in advance, Katie.